LITTLE WRITER

MARINA HILL

EVERGREEN
BOOKS

For
readers of color who love historical fiction

Author's Note

I've debated with myself for months whether to add this note, but I think its inclusion will be beneficial.

I implement all of the characters' written descriptions in *Little Women*. However, in *Little Writer*, Jo, Meg, Amy, Beth, and Marmee are black, Laurie Laurence is of Asian descent, and John Brooke is of Native American descent. While the characters in *Little Writer* are multiracial, that is all I include regarding their identity.

You could say they live in a raceless world—or in alternate history, as some like to say.

I know both people of color and white people who disagree with literature that implements this method of storytelling. But I firmly stand by my decision to do this.

The history of people of color in the United States is long, brutal, and ugly. There are certainly pockets of joy, but it was rarely documented.

Readers of color who love historical fiction struggle with finding a book where they *don't* suffer because of their racial identity. Black people are constantly reminded of those who hate us, i.e. the massacre in Buffalo, New York. Racism is debilitating and exhausting.

I want readers of color to escape the hatred when reading this book; racism will still exist outside of the pages.

CHAPTER 1

THE BOY ACROSS THE WAY

Mud squelches around my feet and lines the hem of my skirt. Meg is going to *kill* me.

I suppose sisterly devotion is to blame; Beth's forlorn expressions take hold of my heart every time. She loves these dear kittens, and I sacrifice my cleanliness to find them each time they run away. Wiggling my toes beneath water-logged socks, I survey the unkempt garden and consider my predicament. Another glance at the soiled blue fabric of my clothes confirms I have nothing more to lose. With a sigh, I drop to my hands and knees.

"Here kitty, kitty," I grumble, crawling around the muck in search of the tiny black cat in question. Beth's cats seldom cause good in the family, for Meg threatens to have them drowned whenever she's in a sour mood, and they're always after my pet mouse—Scrabble.

A quick peek under the usual garden plants proves fruitless. "Beth's worried. Come out, come out..." The downpour from last night makes the search harder. The frigid mud coating my hands and wrists elicit a loud *squelch* with every movement. "Pst pst pst." I continue beckoning for the mischievous animal until my lips become chapped and, as a closing punishment, the thick braid down my back falls over my shoulder, bedraggling the tip in mud.

"Fairy godmother," I mutter, staring up at the sky, "please grant me a wish."

"Looking for this?" a voice interrupts.

My head jerks aside as a startled "fairy godmother?" escapes my lips. But when I squint past the wooden gate, I see a boy who couldn't be much older than I. He observes me with a curious look. I suppose I should feel embarrassed, but my attention settles on the furry bundle in his arms.

Beth's kitty! This boy is my fairy godmother after all. "You found her!" I exclaim, scrambling to my feet, but my foot catches on my skirt and yanks me back to the ground. With a yelp, my hands splash into the mud and flick specks onto my cheeks. *Very unladylike*, as Amy would chide. When I rise, I wipe my hands on my clothes and fly toward the gate.

"I found her under the rocking chair on our porch," the boy says. His black eyes trail over my mud-coated outfit as I scoop up the wad of fur.

"Oh, thank you! I was going to drive myself mad looking for her." I study the boy's dark curly hair and the light freckles dancing little jigs over his brown nose, and realize we've not yet been acquainted. "Where do you live?"

He gestures behind him, and my eyes fall upon the enormous house across the way; the very one my sisters and I gossip about.

"That's *your* house?"

The boy reddens and gives a small nod. "I live there with my grandfather."

I let out a low whistle, which sends the boy's face into a deep crimson. "You must have a capital time in that mansion!" The stately residence contrasts with our plain, brown house, and I possess a sudden awareness of my brown-spattered frock. How dreadfully improper I must look...

He shrugs.

A frown tugs at my lips as I wrestle the kitten wriggling to free itself from my grip. Surely anyone living in that house would be lifting their chin and yelling it from the rooftops. I can only dream of the luxuries he must have.

"It's okay," he adds as if reading my thoughts. "I study most of the time."

"Do you have a library?"

For the first time, his mouth curves into a smile. "Yes, I—"

He's interrupted yet again, only this time it's by my older sister Meg yelling from inside the house. "*Jo!* Jo, where are you!"

I spin around in a huff, my wet braid thwacking my cheek. "Give me a minute!" I screech. But when I turn back, the boy is already leaving. "Wait!" He only continues walking across the field, back hunched, without so much as a glance in my direction. I pierce him with a glare he can't see, then hold up the kitten as if touting an award and offer a final cry. "I'm taking the credit!" With that, I whirl around and run toward the house, arms still extended and holding up the fussy prize. "Beth, look what I found!"

The back door swings shut behind Meg as she stands frozen with a blanched face. *"What have you done to your clothes!"*

THE FOLLOWING WEEK, MEG AND I WALK SIDE BY SIDE down the snowy roads; my cloak is no match for the December chill. I cling tighter to my older sister's arm for warmth as the mansion up ahead draws into view. My curiosity leaps at the sight of the boy from before as he shovels the grand walkway.

"It's you!" I call excitedly, dashing to the gate.

Turning in surprise, he offers a simple smile before hitching his shovel in a mound of snow. Is he so humble he doesn't use servants for that kind of work? "Hi," he says, walking closer and rubbing together his gloved hands. His hair puffs out from beneath his hat.

"D'you want help?" I nod toward the shovel. "I'm rather good at shov—"

"Josephine!"

Meg appears at my side and rethreads her arm through mine. She shoots the boy a hesitant look before tugging me along to end a jolly time before it could even begin. "Stop that," she scolds, smothering a cough from her lingering cold. She clears her throat. "You don't know him."

"But—"

"Let's *go*." Her stern look tells me it's not up for discussion.

As she drags me toward home—rather skillfully, as she can curtail my resistance and carry a big basket of cooking ingredients for Hannah at the same time—I look back to the boy. A despondent countenance replaces his amused curiosity. The sight tugs at my heart, and I wish I could run over to keep him company. I misunderstood his earlier indifference—the cavalier dismissal of his stately house, his stately wealth, his stately library. He's lonely.

I give him a small wave. He returns the gesture.

By Jove, I swear I'll come to know that boy!

CHAPTER 2

A SOLDIER IN SOCKS

I wiggle my toes in my socks, eyes shut. Greediness captures me as I grumble, "Christmas won't be Christmas without gifts."

Meg sits in Mother's reading chair as she knits. "Being poor is so dreadful."

"It's not fair for some people to have heaps of expensive things and some none at all," says my youngest sister Amy, who always wants frivolous, unimportant belongings rather than simple necessities. If my eyes were open, I'd roll them.

But Beth, my ever-loving, gentle sister, says, "We've got family."

"Not Father," I blurt. "Not for a long time." Right away, I regret my words because Beth upsets easily. But I can't help the sadness that floods through me at the possibility of him never coming home. Is he okay? What's it like on the battlefield? Is it cold and dreadful? It's likely much different from the forceful heat pulsing from the fireplace to my right.

Meg's mother-like voice cuts into my thoughts. "Mother said no presents this Christmas because it'll be a hard winter, and she thinks we shouldn't spend money for pleasure when our men suffer in the army. We can't do much, but we can make that sacrifice."

Puh, how ludicrous! As women, our sacrifice for the country is giving up whatever makes us happy! I roll onto my stomach and open my eyes before releasing a sardonic scoff. "What good does that do? *Oh, no! I can't dirty my shoes and wield a weapon, so I guess I'll give up my new gloves!*" I scoff. "It's insulting."

Amy groans from her spot curled up on the couch. "Jo, no one wants to hear your lecture on women's rights today. Put the pitchfork down."

"Never!" I say. "Our money is our own." Eager to inspire my sisters to be more selfish, I sit up with a melodramatic flourish. We labor for others much too often! It's time to take a cut for ourselves. "Ames, don't you want more paper for sketching? You could—*Christopher Columbus!*" Meg throws a pillow at my head.

"Stop it, Jo," she says.

"And stop using such slang words," Amy adds.

Stop this, stop that. Nothing I do is satisfactory for them! Shadows of insecurity hover around me, but I shrug them off and jump to my feet. Sliding my hands into the pockets of my robe, I wander around the parlor and begin whistling. This angers my sisters even more and seems to disgust Amy.

"Don't, Jo. It's so boyish!"

"That's why I do it," I bark spitefully.

She leans forward, flat nose in the air. "I detest rude, unladylike girls!"

I step closer and stick my tongue out. "And I hate affected, niminy-piminy chits!"

From beside Amy, Beth takes my arm and draws me to her side, singing, "*Birds in their little nests agree.*" It softens my heart as I lower beside her. Beth often pushes herself into the middle of sister arguments because none of us can get angry at her.

"Both of you are wrong," Meg lectures, then looks at me with her stern blue eyes. "You're old enough to stop your boyish tricks and behave better, Josephine. You're not a little girl anymore, but now tall and turn up your hair. Remember to be a young lady."

I can't help groaning as I drape my legs across Beth's lap. I'm always the first of the family to take criticism. Not Amy and her vanity. Not Meg and her lack of a spine. Not Beth and her shyness. I rip off my bonnet and let my wild, chestnut curls puff around my face and fall to my stomach.

"But I'm *not* a lady. I'll be a crotchety old woman with long hair and dirty dresses! If not wanting to look as prim as a China Aster makes me boyish, then so be it! I would much rather go and fight with Papa."

Beth tugs me closer and strokes my hair. "Poor Jo. It can't be helped, so try to be content with a boyish name and being our brother figure."

My fellow middle sister is the one who gives me the most sympathy. I can't help who I am—that I like "boyish" games and manners. December snow falls outside as the sound of crackling fire echoes through the house. We have quite a plain home, but it always holds such vibrant energies they pour out the windows because they can't fit. My books rest in the vacant corner of the parlor and I long to swipe one and crawl to the attic for evening reading.

But, in the silence, Beth exclaims, "It's six! Mother should be home soon!"

Struck with sudden energy, we leap up and scramble to make the place inviting for Marmee. My sisters bustle behind me as I take Marmee's slippers and hold them closer to the blazing fire. The slippers have a small hole at the big toe that I ought to tell Meg to sew up, but my mother will be home any moment. Oh, I can't wait until I'm a successful and famous writer! That way, my family never has to suffer a torn slipper or stained skirt again. The thought of successful writing reminds me of the Christmas play.

"Meg!" I shout. "We must go shopping tomorrow afternoon. We have much to do before the play."

"Oh—Jo!" Meg appears behind me, her hands tangling in my curls. I try to shake her off. She braids my hair in a swift motion. "What have I told you about letting your hair dangle near the fire? And all right, but after this, I'm done acting. I'm getting too old."

I smother a laugh. "You're not done. As long as you can prance around in a white gown with your hair down and wear gold paper jewelry, you'll adore being our star actress."

"*Jo...*" Meg drawls.

I peer over my shoulder at her. "You love it. Don't act like you don't." I set the slippers down and jump to my feet. "Ames! Come practice the fainting scene. You're too stiff."

My sisters don't often have kind things to say to me, aside from Beth, but they praise my writing. It is my strongest skill and biggest contribution to the family. In every other aspect, I'm an embarrassment.

"I can't help it!" Amy whines as I situate her in front of me. "I've never seen anyone faint and I won't make myself all black and blue, tumbling as you do. I'll fall into a chair and be graceful and I don't care if Hugo comes at me with a pistol." She flips her honey-gold curls. "I wish he would. I'll scare him with my glare."

A laugh bubbles in my throat. "Okay—do it this way." I clasp my hands and begin staggering about the room, knocking into Beth as I pretend to lose consciousness. "Roderigo! Save me! Save me!"

My chest swells with pride as Meg beams at my performance. Amy tries to mimic, but she pokes her stiff hands in front of her and jerks along as if she had a string tethered to her waist. I slap my hand against my forehead and collapse onto the couch. Meg laughs.

Beth grins and points at me. "Like that! Do what Jo just did and you'll be great!"

"It's no use," I grumble. "Just do the best you can. Don't blame me if the audience laughs." I grab Meg's wrist, pulling her into rehearsal for the next half hour. It passes somewhat smoothly until she tries to die before actually being poisoned with the arsenic. "No, no! Not yet! You can't do things out of order; the audience won't understand! Stick to how the story goes."

Meg sits up and rubs her elbows. "Relax, Jo. We'll get it in time."

Beth pokes the logs and adds more wood. I sigh and rub the crease out of my eyebrows. This is my contribution to the family; it *must* be great.

"I know, I know."

Beth wraps her arms around me and plants her chin on my shoulder. "I don't understand how you can write and act such splendid things, Jo." She pecks my cheek. "You're a regular Shakespeare!"

My face warms, but I sober up and untangle myself from her arms to pace the room with my hands clasped behind my back and chin held high. "Not quite. I'd like to try *Macbeth*, if we only had a trapdoor for Banquo. I always wanted to do the killing part." My expression fades as I reach into midair and let my eyes roll back. *"Is—is that a dagger that I see before me?"*

"No," Meg responds, "it's the toasting fork with Mother's shoe on the other end."

We all erupt in laughter, only stopping when seeing Marmee in the doorway saying, "Glad to find my girls so merry."

"Marmee!" we exclaim, rushing to her side and helping take off her wet cloak, gloves, and hat.

"Well, well," Mother says with a laugh. "How did you all get along today? There was so much to do, getting the boxes ready to go."

"We've got it covered!" I say as she slips her shoes off in exchange for her warmed slippers. "So—do you have it? Did he write?"

A few weeks ago, Beth said she had a feeling Papa would be writing to us soon. Her premonitions are almost always right, so we'd been asking Marmee about it each time she arrives home. Beth clutches my wrist with anxiety as we all await her answer. My mother nods and says, "Yes, yes, but we'll read it after dinner. Let me relax first." Marmee extends her hands toward Meg. "How's your cold, dear?"

I hustle to the kitchen and gather a tea tray. I manage to drop and over-turn and clatter almost everything I touch. It isn't until I reach the end table does Marmee reach out to me.

"You look tired to death, baby. Come kiss me."

After dinner, she brings us into the parlor for us to gather around her chair. I stay in the back so I can slip away if I begin crying.

As Marmee reads, I close my eyes and hear the words in Papa's voice and imagine myself beside him.

I look up and I'm sitting on a cot inside a tent. I'm still wearing my shift and thin mantle. Papa walks inside and grins, his bright teeth splitting his bushy beard in two.

"Papa!" I exclaim, jumping up and throwing my arms around him. "Oh, I miss you."

"I miss you, too, my little writer. Come, let me show you the camp."

He takes my hand and guides me outside. The sun blinds me and horses stomp by and men chitter. The damp ground seeps through my socks and soaks my feet. None of that matters. His arm wraps around me and I savor the warmth of his embrace. He points at a group of men standing around a table inside an open tent. "They're deciding where the soldiers will march." Then he gestures toward men crowding around a fire. "They're having lunch." Papa leads me through the crowd and a couple of them nod at me in acknowledgment. My toes turn numb at the cold and wiggling them does no good. He opens a creaky door to a wooden shack. There are four beds and some candles that barely light the entire place. "And this is where I sleep."

At the sight of the threadbare blankets and the shiver running over my body, I look at him with bewildered eyes. "Aren't you cold at night?"

Papa smiles a gentle smile that I miss dearly. His silver hair, his thick beard, his soft hands. I miss my papa and I can't wait until he comes home.

"I'm all right, my dear." He takes my hands in his and kisses my knuckles. "Give your sisters my love. Tell them I think of you all by day, pray for you by night, and find my best comfort in your affection at all times. A year seems so long to wait to see you, but we will work in the meantime." He pokes my nose with the tip of his finger. "These hard days won't be wasted. Be loving children for your mother and remember all I've said to you. Do your duties faithfully, fight your enemies bravely, and conquer them beautifully so that I can be even more proud of my little women when I return."

Tears stream down my face as I throw my hands around his neck and squeeze my eyes shut. "Oh, we will, Papa. I love you." By the time my eyes flutter open, I'm back to leaning on the chair, my body warm, my feet dry, and my heart aching for my father.

CHAPTER 3

LOVE ON CHRISTMAS MORNING

I'm the first to rise on Christmas morning.

After sliding on an extra pair of socks and wiggling the feeling back into my toes, I slip out of the bed Meg and I share and creep downstairs. Slight disappointment fills me at the limp stockings hanging on the fireplace, for they used to fall to the ground from being so crammed with goodies.

I wade through the quiet house alight with white-yellow hues illuminating dust in its rays. Hannah, who cooks breakfast in the kitchen, quirks a brow when I retrieve gifts from my hidden compartment under the sink.

"What ye doin'?" she asks as she stirs a wooden spoon in a pot.

"Nothing!" I chirp, cradling the gifts in my hands as I kiss her pale cheek. "Merry Christmas, Hannah."

"Merry Christmas, dear. Your ma will be back soon—she said to open the gifts without her."

"Where'd she go?"

Hannah waves a hand. "Go wake yer sisters first."

With my brown-and-orange mantle billowing behind me, I flee the kitchen. When I place my family's gifts under the tree, I spot presents marked with my and my sisters' names. The sight sends joy shuddering through my heart and a gasp to my lips. I dart upstairs and leap onto the bed.

"Wake up! Wake up! It's Christmas!"

Meg's body flops from my jumping as Amy and Beth stir awake. "Jo!" she groans. "Stop it." I fall on top of her. "Josephine!" She thrashes me and I laugh when she tries to toss me away. "Get off me!"

I stop and wait for her eyes to open and see my smiling face. "We have presents."

Her irritation vanishes and her mouth falls. "Really?"

"We have gifts?" Amy asks, sitting up and rubbing the sleep from her eyes. The sunlight from the window behind her outlines her body as if she were an angel.

"Hannah said Marmee's out and wants us to open the gifts without her. Come and see!"

My sisters trample behind me into the parlor where we crash at the bottom of the tree. The fire blazes, its soft heat buzzing on my skin, but my heart is full of enough warmth to last me through any winter. Christmas morning snow falls softly outside, blanketing the world in white. We sit in a semicircle— Meg and Amy in their silk nightcaps, Beth and I letting our wild curls frizz around our faces—and pass around gifts to each respective recipient.

Meg's hands hover over her stack of gifts in anticipation. "Okay, ready?"

"One," says Amy, beginning our countdown. Excitement radiates from her body in the form of shining eyes and tight shoulders.

"Two," says Beth patiently.

I hesitate for dramatic effect. "*Three!*"

We all rip into our presents at the same time, *oohing* and *aahing* at what we unravel. Unlike the other girls who have two gifts each, I only have one. But I'm satisfied enough with Friedrich de la Motte Fouqué's *Undine*—a fairytale book I've been wanting!

"Yes!" I shout, shaking the book like the winner of a grand prize.

"Faber's drawing pencils!" Amy exclaims.

"Oh—new gloves!" Meg screeches, holding them to her heart.

Beth stares at the music sheets. "Beethoven music sheets!"

Aside from the gifts I bought them, we each receive a book from Marmee. "We all have a book! Remember, Marmee wants us all to start reading more," says Meg. "We won't let her down."

Beth looks up at me, and upon seeing the book in my lap, her joy fades. "Why do you only have one gift and we have two?"

A smile tugs at my lip but I feign nonchalance, shrugging my reply. "I don't know."

"Jo—did you buy us this?" Meg asks, her expression serious and tone grave.

On a regular day, it takes immense effort for me to be sentimental. Today, I have to kick away the love threatening to bubble up in tears. Meg's work as a governess exhausts her, Amy struggles in school, and Papa's absence on Christmas leaves Beth feeling rather blue. I ache to contribute more than writing to this family, and Marmee was happy to help me weave in more happiness for my sisters.

"Aunt March paid me extra to clean her dusty attic with all those nasty spiders and I saved every penny! Marmee helped me pick them out. Do you like them?"

A beat of silence passes as they exchange glances. Amy squeals, "Oh—Jo!" and dives across Beth. She tackles me in a hug as laughter escapes me. "It's just what I wanted!" she cries. "Thank you, thank you, thank you! You're the best sister!"

Meg and Beth jump into the hug and pile on top of me, regardless of knowing hugs are not my preferred method of affection. Embraces usually make me feel trapped, but joy blossoms in my chest. The luxuries I may buy myself will never compare to the satisfaction of giving those I love a gift they've been yearning for.

"We love you!" Beth says and kisses my curly head over and over.

"I'm sorry for all the dreadful things I've said to you, dear!" says Meg, kissing my cheek.

"Okay, okay—too much love," I grumble as the hug dissipates.

Amy orders, "Oh, Beth, go get it! Go get it!" and my younger sister flees the room.

"Get what?" I ask and adjust my robe in an attempt to shake off my usual discomfort for embraces.

Meg, ever the motherly sister, runs her hands over my hair to soothe my growing suspicions. "We know how seriously you take the stories you write for us. We want you to know how much we love it and how much we love *you*"—she offers me a sly smile—"no matter how boyish you may act."

I pull my hair over one shoulder and roll my eyes at her implication that acting less feminine makes me any less worthy of love. "You bought me a gift?"

"We want you to keep getting inspired," Amy says, snatching the gift from Beth.

I smother a frown and reach up toward Beth to draw her to my side. The windows groan with the frigid breeze outside, but the crackling fire beside the Christmas tree offers warmth. I curse the tears welling in my eyes when I split open the brown wrapping paper. "Oh..." I breathe. Two oversized tears spill down my cheek as I brush my fingers over the copy of Friedrich de la Motte Fouqué's other famous work, *Sintram and His Companions*.

Amy jostles Beth with her elbow and says smugly, "Told you she would cry."

"*Shh*," Beth hushes and wraps her arms around me and leans her head on my shoulder. "Do you like it?"

"I *love* it."

Meg tugs on one of my curls. "Keep writing, Jo, and be the *best* writer the world has ever seen."

A grin stretches over my face. It's not even eight o'clock in the morning, and this is the *best* Christmas. "Thank you. I have the most amazing sisters in the world!"

Meg jumps up and makes for the dining room. "Merry Christmas, Hannah!"

"Where's Marmee?" Beth asks as she helps me to my feet.

We pick up the wrapping paper and place our gifts neatly under the tree. My mouth waters at the aroma of bacon and apple cider. When we dance through the yellow hues of the morning sun cutting through the dining room windows, Hannah says, "Some poor creeter came a-beggin,' and your ma when straight off to help."

"She'll be back soon, so let's get everything ready!" I exclaim. We part ways to gather the gifts we bought for Mother. After this Christmas, I've not a single penny left in my money sock.

"Where on earth is Amy?" Meg later asks, crossing her arms over her dark brown mantle. She could have begged for a new robe the way Amy always does, but she meekly accepted Marmee's old one. It's rather irksome the way my older sister *never* puts her own desires first, but I suppose she has a journey of lessons ahead as I do.

"Not a clue." I trample about the room, breaking in the new army slippers for Marmee.

Beth holds up the handkerchiefs she marked and beams with pride. "Look at how nice my handkerchiefs are! Hannah washed and ironed them for me."

I pluck one from her grasp as I twirl around the room, letting out a giggle when I read her handiwork. "Oh, you've gone and put *Mother* on them instead of *M. March!* How funny!"

"I don't want anyone else to use them," she explains, a frown painting her brown face. "Marmee and Meg have the same initial."

Meg snatches the handkerchief from me with a warning glare and flattens it on the table. "There," she says, stepping back to admire the smooth cloth. She places her arm on Beth's shoulder, who dons a worried expression. "It's a good idea, dear, and very pretty! Marmee will be so pleased."

"I'm here, I'm here!" Amy shouts as she rushes into the room with her arms behind her back.

"Where have you been?" I scold, taking off the slippers to place them with the other gifts. "Marmee will be here any minute!"

Amy's face reddens and she turns her blue eyes to the ground. "Well—I'm trying not to be selfish anymore, so I used up the last of my money to switch out the little bottle for a big one." She reveals the handsome flask that replaced the cheap one, earning a collective gasp.

"Amy, you didn't!" Beth says before enveloping her younger sister in a hug.

After we take turns praising her, Amy adds, "I felt ashamed of my present and I wanted it to be good. And I'm glad I did it, for mine is the handsomest now."

I arch a brow as Meg sets Amy's new gift among the rest. "Ames—wanting your gift to be the best out of ours is the... opposite of being selfless."

She sticks her tongue out and blows a raspberry. Before I can do the same, the front door opens and we all rush to welcome Marmee. "Merry Christmas!" we croon, gathering around and bringing her to the kitchen for breakfast while thanking her for the books.

"Merry Christmas, my dears!" She kisses each of us. "Before we start," Marmee says with a sigh. She brushes a lock from her face. Despite the sadness lingering behind her eyes, a smile brightens her dark skin. "Not far away from here lies Mrs. Hummel, a poor, sick woman with a newborn baby. She has six children huddled into one bed to keep from freezing and they have no fire. They have no food. They are cold and hungry. Oh, my dears, will you give them your breakfast as a Christmas present?"

Silence cloaks the dining room. My stomach aches for breakfast and rumbles louder at the possibility of giving it away. Marmee has always been so generous. My sisters and I exchange wary glances. None of us wants to give up our food, but Marmee says a family needs it more—so I chirp, "I'm so glad you came before we started!"

Everyone jumps into motion. Beth tugs Marmee's arm and asks, "May I go and help carry the things to the poor little children?"

I rush to the kitchen to grab our extra baskets. We scramble to dress and prepare and we're soon out the door, swerving through back roads to get there sooner. As we part through the woods, my pace slows so I can savor the gentle snowfall. The sun peeks between the branches and I hesitate when a bird flutters across the ray of light. For a moment, I think the wings belong to a fairy, for the sparkling snow can be mistaken for fairy dust.

"Fairies in the trees," I whisper with my arms wrapped

around the basket of quilts. "Fairies twirl through trees and with leaves for wings and sticks as wands."

I repeat the words in my head; I must remember to write them down when I return home. When we reach the shack, I halt. Imagination flees my mind as I'm overcome with dreadful realization. My chest tightens at the broken windows and slabs of wood missing from the walls—and they *live* in this.

"Jo, dear?" Marmee asks with a concerned look.

I gulp thinking of how little time I can bear to be in the cold, and yet... "They *live* here?"

She purses her lips. "Yes." Yesterday, we complained about being poor. Now, I want to hug and thank my mother for the life we have. She places a hand on my back and guides me forward. "We're here to do good. Remember that."

I inhale and nod. Inside is a bare room with no fires, ragged clothes, a crying baby, a sick mother, and blue, hungry children cuddling under a quilt. Marmee is the only one of us who moves. My sisters and I stand frozen; none of us knew that people live like this. Marmee picks up the crying baby and directs the mother to lie down. When she looks over her shoulder, she hisses, "*Girls.*"

As if struck, we spring into action. I set the basket of quilts on the table and begin taking them out. Meg takes the baby from Marmee and Marmee takes the basket of medicines to tend to Mrs. Hummel. Beth takes to the unloading the food and Amy sets up the plates and I wrap the children in as many blankets as I can.

"Hi, I'm Jo," I say to a little girl as I place a hat on her head and warm her blue hands in mine.

She sniffles, snot inching out of her nose. "*Ich heiße* Anna."

Meg appears at my side, swaddling the newborn who has since stopped crying. She rubs a cloth under Anna's nose to clean the snot. "That means *my name is*," she says to me. "*Hallo,*

Anna, *ich heiße* Meg. *Das ist meine Familie,* Amy, *und* Beth. *Hast du Hunger?*"

I lift my brow at Meg; she tends to the children as if it's natural to her. She shrugs at my disbelieving stare. "The Kings have been teaching me a little German. That's about all I know," she admits.

I smile. "You're going to make a great mother one day."

A blush rises to her cheeks as she takes Anna's hand and guides her to the dining table. For the next hour, we serve and we laugh and we comfort and it's the most satisfying morning I've ever experienced despite the grumbling of my stomach. The joy of giving is much more fulfilling than the joy of receiving. By the time we leave, my family and I are happier than we've been all month.

CHAPTER 4

A GRAND PLAY

Magic ensues every time writing comes to life. Soul and heart live in each word, dazzling the crowd as the speaker immortalizes the writer. Glitter will flutter and mouths will smile. When villains unsheathe their swords and declare their wishes, heads will bend and whisper to one another.

A twinkle will shimmer in the audience's eyes, for a good villain is much agreeable for the sake of the story. But, alas! The heroes will prosper every time.

Love sprinkles through the grand theater. The Christmas night festivities dance. Come hither from thy home, for the hero needs affection, and none other will do than the woman he sets his eyes upon. Glittering wings sway as the golden-haired maiden dances into view.

I stand offstage and peek around the curtain with my fingers laced together tightly. I watch the thousands of impassioned faces reacting to the story. Relief shudders through my chest. They're enjoying the show.

A hand grips my shoulder. *"You did it,"* they whisper.

When the curtains rise and my cast bows, they turn to me. Proud smiles and deafening claps greet me as I bow before the crowd. They praise the writer. My immortality is promised.

CHAPTER 5

THE LAURENCES

When the play is over and we've bid the audience of family friends farewell, I run into the dining room at Amy's dramatic gasp.

"Is it fairies?" Amy asks and my eyes widen at the decorated dinner table. There's ice cream and cake and fruit and bonbons and a huge bouquet of flowers! I salivate at the sight.

"Santa Claus," Beth whispers in amazement.

"Whatever it is, I don't care," I say and plop into my usual seat. My fingers twitch. Where does one even *start* with such an array of options?

Meg lowers beside me and removes her fake gray beard. She pulls her braid over her shoulder to tighten the ribbon at the end. "Don't be silly. Mother did it."

Marmee spreads her napkin over her lap and says, "All wrong. Old Mr. Laurence sent it."

I begin stuffing my face with bread rolls while my sisters share their theories about the mysterious mansion next door. Our family is bound to be acquainted with the Laurences. "That boy put it into his head," I muffle. "I know he did. He—"

"Don't talk with your mouth full," Amy scolds.

I take another bite and keep talking. "He's a capital fellow, and I wish we could get acquainted. He's shy and Meg is so prim she doesn't let me talk to him when we pass."

Meg elbows me. "Well, who keeps their grandson locked up like that, anyway? Doesn't seem like someone we should know."

"I like his manners and he looks like a little gentleman," Marmee says. "I've no objection to knowing him. He brought the flowers himself and seemed as though he wanted to join. I should have asked him in."

Amy frowns. "That would mean sharing."

Marmee raises a brow and speaks pointedly. "And we're okay with sharing."

When Amy reddens, I say, "He found Beth's black cat when she ran away. He didn't even look at me funny when I was all covered in mud! We talked over the fence and got along capitally until he saw Meg. I mean to know him one day, for I'm sure he needs fun."

My attempt to ease her embarrassment backfires since I all but forgot that I'd taken the credit for the Laurence boy's discovery. Beth tilts her head and asks, "I thought *you* were the one who found Whiskers?"

My family looks at me with questioning eyes and Amy giggles from across the table. Instead of replying, I stuff my face with as much food as I can. They don't want me to talk with my mouth full!

THE BRIGHT SUN STREAMING THROUGH THE ATTIC windows doesn't dry my tears as I wish it would. The emotional scenes of *The Heir of Redclyffe* never fail to remind me I'm nothing but a measly human with feelings I cannot control.

"Jo! Jo, are you up there?" Meg calls from the bottom of the garret stairs.

I flinch, tossing the book and wiping off the tears as fast as I can. "Up here!" my husky voice says. Curse these emotions.

She runs up the stairs and I bite one of my apple slices to help swallow the emotion clogging my throat. Meg reaches the landing and at the same time, Scrabble scurries across her feet.

She yelps. "Oh, for—Jo!"

"Scrabble's harmless," I remind and attempt to finger-comb my matted curls. "What's the news?"

She shudders. "I don't understand how you—never mind." She holds up a piece of paper and squeals with a big grin spreading over her brown face. "We have an invitation to a dance on New Year's Eve at Mrs. Gardiner's! Marmee is letting us." She flies forward and takes my hands, dragging me toward the stairs. "Oh—what shall we wear?"

I groan and call over my shoulder, "Don't touch my apples, Scrabble!"

"He's a rat, for God's sake," Meg scolds as we trample down the stairs to our bedroom. After some quarreling, I finally agree to attend and be on my best behavior. It would be in bad taste if only one invitee shows up, so I tuck away my irritation on New Year's Eve and dress in the best clothes I have. To Meg's horror, my best skirt has a burn stain.

Beth is finalizing some of the nineteen pins poking into my head as I stare at myself in the mirror. I touch the sides of my wide nostrils and push in. My nose, flatter than the noses of most girls I know, carries insecurity when I allow it. Every woman in my family has similar wide noses, much to Amy's chagrin.

"Why do you hate these parties so much?" Beth asks in a soft voice.

I sigh. "Because I... I'm not good at how a lady is supposed to act and these parties point that out. And I embarrass whoever I'm with."

Silence follows for moments as she finishes my hair and fluffs my skirt. She rests her chin on my shoulder and stares at me through the mirror, the candlelight illuminating her round face. Her full lips curve into a soft smile as her light brown curls fall over my shoulder.

"You're not the problem, Jo. Society is."

I attempt a smile and rest my head on hers. "Thanks."

We walk downstairs to meet Meg and Amy who wait with such impatience at the door. "What took you so long?" asks Amy with a worried air—as if she's coming with us. "You'll be late!"

Meg blanches. "Where are your gloves?"

I wave my hand. "Oh—spoiled with lemonade. I can't get any new ones, so I shall have to go without."

"Oh, *no!*" she wails, then flies upstairs.

"You can't go without gloves," Amy tells me, flipping her hair over her shoulder. "Gloves are more important than anything else." She turns to Mother. "See, Marmee! This is why *I* should be going with Meg—not Jo!"

"You weren't invited," I snap as I secure a loose pin in my hair.

"Girls." Marmee appears in the threshold leading to the parlor with hands on her hips. She speaks in a calm tone, but with enough edge to warn us not to get into a scrape. I'm bound to embarrass Meg tonight so it's best I keep out of sight as much as possible. This is the part where I'm *not* great at contributing to the family.

Meg stomps back downstairs, slightly breathless, with an old pair in hand. "Here's my old pair. Now, I'm wearing the ones you bought me. *Don't* ruin this pair, Jo. I mean it."

I touch my fingers to my forehead and salute despite

knowing I'm bound to disappoint. Prim and proper with dance cards and feather fans—none of these descriptions can apply to me. My family tries to force them to.

As we head down the walkway, Mother calls from the door, "Have a good time, dearies! Don't eat much supper. I'll send Hannah for you at eleven!" We are mere steps away from leaving earshot when she adds, "Oh—girls, girls! Do you both have nice pocket handkerchiefs?"

Meg and I yell in unison, "Yes, Marmee!"

"She would ask that if we were running from an earthquake," I mumble, wrapping my cloak tighter about me.

She giggles. "Yes, but it's one of her aristocratic tastes. It's quite proper, for a real lady is always known by neat boots, gloves, and handkerchief. Now, remember, no putting your hands behind your back, no saying *Christopher Columbus*, and no shaking hands with anyone you're introduced to. It's not the thing anymore."

"This is too much information," I say. We pass under lighted oil lamps along the snowy street. My boots crunch over the frozen snow. "Just wink at me if you see me doing something wrong."

Meg shakes her head. "No, that's not ladylike. I'll lift my eyebrows if anything is wrong, and nod if you are all right." She squeezes my hand. "You can do this—I believe in you."

I want to stick my tongue out and blow a raspberry. This night is already dreadful, but I shall do my best to improve the March name. Mrs. Gardiner, a sweet old lady, greets us at the front door and hands us off to one of her six daughters. Meg, who already knows Sallie, disappears with her friend. I find a comfortable wall to press my back to. A group of boys chatting about skating passes me. I move toward their conversation until Meg catches my eye and throws her brows up into her hairline. I huff and retreat to the wall. I can't prance about as I wish to, for my burned skirt is much too obvious.

A red-headed boy stares at me. My stomach tingles with anticipation and my throat tightens with dread when he starts in my direction. *No, stay over there!* The tossing of glances across the crowded room is more than enough for me. I slip between the curtains so I can observe in peace. A person bumps into me once I back into the study.

"Christopher Columbus!" When I look up, I see it's the Laurence boy! "Oh, I didn't know you were here! Well—here at the party and here-here." He watches me with a bashful face; I shift at his awkward silence and add, "I'll just—I'll leave—"

"Oh—no!" he stammers, gesturing toward a seat. "Don't mind me. Stay—if you like."

I bite the inside of my cheek and tug on the dance card around my wrist. "I shan't disturb you?"

He shakes his head and folds his hands behind his back. "Not a bit. I only came here because I don't know many people and felt rather strange at first."

"So did I!" I exclaim and snatch his arm to drag him toward the seats. "Don't go away, please." I lower myself into a chair and watch him until he sits beside me. Seconds tick by and he remains silent. I clear my throat. "You still haven't told me your name, Mr. Laurence."

"I—I'm not Mr. Laurence. Only Laurie, Miss March."

I smile. "And I'm not Miss March—I'm only Jo."

Amusement flickers in his eyes, his shyness dissipating as the moments pass between us. "Jo," he repeats as if testing it out. "What an odd name."

"*Laurie Laurence.* Also an odd name."

Laurie laughs, his smile brightening his freckled brown skin. "My first name is Theodore, but I don't like it. My friends tried to call me Dora, and I like that even less, so I settled on Laurie."

"Well, that's insensible," I snort. "Did you not consider Teddy in your search for a suitable nickname?" He grins again; it's the most emotion I've gotten out of him since our first meeting. "I hate my name too. I wish everyone would say Jo instead of Josephine. How did you make the boys stop calling you Dora?"

The smallest hint of red blots his cheeks. "I thrashed 'em."

"Dear me," I exhale, slumping back into the chair. "It's bad to thrash an old woman, right?"

Laurie barks out a laugh and leans back into his seat. "Yes, Miss Jo. And I believe you know that," he adds with a teasing smirk. "Say, don't you like to dance?"

I stretch my legs and cross my ankles. "I like it well enough if it's not cramped and if the people are interesting. In a place like this, I'm sure to trample on toes and knock something over. So I'm staying out of scrapes and letting Meg sail about." I turn my attention back to the Laurence boy. It's difficult to imagine him thrashing anyone. He's gentle. "What about you? Don't you dance?"

"Sometimes. I've been abroad for a while, but I haven't been into company enough yet to know how you do things here."

"Abroad!" I cry, shooting upright and snatching his arm. The luck of such an event! "Oh, do tell me about it all!"

Laurie sputters at the outburst and is speechless for a few short moments. But I will wait all night for him to gather his composure if it means I learn about life abroad. Presently, he tumbles into tales of school in Vevey, where the boys never wear hats and have a fleet of boats and venture to Switzerland for holiday fun.

I sigh, losing myself in a trance as I wander toward the bookshelves. Books are my only means of travel at the moment. "Don't I wish I'd been there. Did you go to Paris?"

"I spent last winter there."

My hands curl into fists. "Oh, Christopher *Columbus*, this is grand! You can teach me how to improve my French and what the Europeans are like and tell me all about your travels and—what is it?" My rant fades when Laurie's shoulders and head droop. Meg tells me my excitement and dedication can be too much for others to handle, and now I've scared away a new friend. "Too much?" I ask, nose crinkled, fingers twiddling together.

Laurie shakes his head. "No, no it's—*Christopher Columbus*. You see, my tutor, John Brooke... his people are from here, but not in the way yours are. He is Native American, of the Wampanoag Nation, and he taught me that the term *Christopher Columbus* is, er, rather offensive. It's the name of the man who led the invasion of his people's land."

I had no idea a name carries such bad history! An embarrassed blush slithers up my neck, though I do my best to shove it down. "I didn't know that. See? I'm smarter already. We're going to get along great. I suppose you're going to college soon? I always see you reading away at your books."

"Not for a year or two. I'm only fifteen. I'll be sixteen next month."

I plop onto an empty corner of the desk. "How I wish I was going to college! You don't look as though you like the idea."

"I hate it!" He grimaces and rises to his feet. "I don't like the way education is done in this country."

My excitement begins to fade. I cannot help thinking, *"What a spoiled boy!"* It is already a privilege to go to college, but to have enough gall to say you hate it! I would love to poke at him about it, but we've only just met and it's not wise to get into a scrape and potentially ruin Meg's night. Instead, I sigh and ask, "Then what *do* you like?"

Laurie leans on the surface beside me. "To live in Italy and enjoy myself in my own way."

Silence follows and I find myself getting more cross with each moment. Perhaps it's best if I change the subject altogether. "I believe there's a splendid polka happening. Why don't you go try it?"

Laurie holds his palm up toward me. "If you'll come too."

I bite the inside of my lip. Oh, how Meg would scold me if she saw me dancing with the state of my skirt. "My skirt is burned," I blurt. Dickens, now I've done it! Rather than shying away, I grab the fabric and reveal the burned section. "Well, I've got a bad habit of standing before the fire, so I often burn my clothes and I scorched this one. And though Meg mended it, she told me to keep still so no one would see it. It's okay, you can laugh."

But Laurie doesn't laugh. He examines the fabric for a moment, dark brows cinched. He brushes his fingers over the burned section, then offers his hand. "Never mind that. I'll tell you how we'll manage. There's a long hall out there and we can dance. No one will see us."

My face warms. For the first time, no one laughs at or scolds my reckless ways. For the first time, someone suggests a way to mend my wily manners with a fun idea. A smile rises to my lips.

I place my hand in Laurie's and let him guide me into the lonely hallway. I grow a little insecure at the sight of his fancy gloves against my too-small hand-me-down pair from Meg. He pretends as though it's nothing and we dance and laugh and joke. What I thought would be a boring night ends up being more splendid than I'd imagined. Laurie Laurence is a grand dance teacher and doesn't poke fun at my mishaps. Instead, he declares he likes my way of dancing better. By the time the music is over, we have a new polka routine, filled with intentional stumbles and consistent laughs.

CHAPTER 6

CAUSE FOR LIVING

"I knew you'd hurt your feet in those silly shoes!" I exclaim, standing before Meg, who's slumped in a chair with a throbbing ankle. "I'm sorry, Gigi, but I don't see what we can do, except getting a carriage or stay here all night."

She sighs and rubs her foot. "I can't have a carriage without its ever costing so much!" Her twisted ankle interrupted Laurie's tale about his travels in Heidelberg, but the worried expression on my sister's face removes any irritation I possessed. My gaze wanders around the private room as if an answer is tucked away somewhere. Before I can find one, Meg says, "I suppose we'll wait for Hannah. Run along and bring me coffee, dear. I'm so tired, I can't think!"

I flee the room, grateful for the chance to find someone to send home, for Meg hates asking favors of the wealthy. If I send Laurie to fetch Mother or Hannah, they can discover a solution. I gather a cup of coffee, which I immediately spill to make the front of my skirt as dreadful as the back.

"What a blunderbuss I am!" I exclaim, using the first thing I can find to scrub away the coffee. Too late do I realize it's one of

Meg's gloves—what she explicitly told me *not* to spoil. I groan. "Can I do *anything* right?"

"May I help?" a friendly voice asks. When I whirl around, I find Laurie! He holds a cup of coffee in one hand and a tray of ice in the other. An innocent smile paints his face. "Forgive me for eavesdropping, it seems—"

"You've saved my life, Theodore Laurence," I cry gratefully, flying toward his and grasping his arm. "Please do. Come this way."

Our arrival startles Meg for an unknown reason, considering she'd been expecting my return. With cinched brows, she flicks her eyes to the curtain, which sways as if recently ruffled. I don't ask what worries her; I urge Laurie ahead and sit beside her. Laurie, a natural gentleman, draws up an end table and situates Meg with her coffee and ice. As we wait for Hannah, the three of us chatter away and nibble on bonbons and play a game of "Buzz" at my suggestion—the game where we say *buzz* to replace the number seven and its multiples.

"Twelve," I say.

"Thirteen," Meg says.

"Buzz!" exclaims Laurie.

I clear my throat. "Fifteen."

"Sixteen," says Meg

"*Buzz*-teen," Laurie says with a satisfied smile.

"Eighteen."

"Nineteen," Meg says.

"Twenty."

"Twenty-one—no! Blast it!" I curse. "I'm not good at math!"

They laugh at my blunder. When Hannah arrives, Laurie says his carriage is here, too, and wishes to take us home. Hannah insists we accept, which results in Laurie sitting in the box so Meg can prop her foot during the ride. I begin tugging out the pins in my updo and ruffling my hair.

"I had a capital time tonight!" I exclaim. "Did you?"

Meg sighs and hesitates, adopting a demeanor much different from the past half hour. Her voice is quiet in the darkness. "A capital time, indeed."

AS THE FAMILY GETS READY THIS MORNING, MEG LIMPS around with a wrapped ankle and whines about having to teach spoiled children today. Beth curls on the couch, groaning with a headache. Marmee busies herself with a letter. Hannah is a grump, Amy is stressed over not knowing her lessons, and I knock over an inkstand, break both boot lacings, and sit on my hat! There has never been such a cross family!

"And you're the crossest in it!" Amy yells when I make such declarations.

"Stop all yer whinin'!" Hannah yells, walking into the parlor with a basket. "Catch yer muffs."

Turnovers we call muffs are the thread that strings us together, preventing the family from falling into constant agitation. Hannah tosses one to each of us. Amy catches hers with both hands and munches into it gratefully. Meg catches hers after a couple of juggles to get a firm grip while exclaiming "Hannah!" in a worried tone.

I wave my hands from the other end of the parlor. "Over here!"

When she throws a muff at me, I fumble it entirely and it falls to the ground. Regardless, I lift it like a prize and shout "It's good!" before taking a bite.

Meg and I leave for work and I reach Aunt March's house after trekking through town. I remove my cloak and hat and snowy shoes, longing for another muff. But the first thing I hear is my aunt's shrill voice.

"*Josyphine!*"

"I'm here, Aunt March!" I shout.

"Stop yelling!" she yells. "I've a headache."

I cross the foyer and head into the library, a room she rarely sits in. "Would you like me to make you some tea?"

Aunt March slumps in her chair with a quilt wrapped around her. "Yes, do that."

I bite my tongue at her lack of manners and whirl toward the grand hallway. What a grouchy old woman she is! Once the tea is served and her headache subsides, I step to the bookshelf to pull out the collection of William Belsham's works. But I hesitate at the sight of Uncle March's painting, for it used to hang above the fireplace in the parlor.

"Why is Uncle March's portrait in here?" I ask, looking over my shoulder at my aunt. Nothing about this situation reads normal. Aunt March *never* sits in here.

"This was his favorite room," she says curtly. "I don't see why he shouldn't reside here. Is that all?"

I lower my gaze to the dark green book in my hands, then to the big dictionaries on the corner shelf. Uncle March used to let me build trains and railroads with them. He would teach me Latin in his free time and he fostered my love for adventure by allowing me to study his maps and globes all day. I remember Aunt March scolding him for indulging my educational interests.

"She has a restless spirit the world won't accept," he replied. *"I want this place to be a region of bliss for her."*

I inhale and shake off the memories wrapping around my heart. My peppery old aunt doesn't allow herself sentiment of any kind, but I say, "I miss him, too," and lower on the sofa across from her. Clearing my throat, I tuck my legs under me and begin reading. Belsham's works are often too intelligent for me to understand, but I hesitate when reaching a certain section. *"Whatever begins to exist must have an adequate cause of its existence; for if the smallest particle of dust, or the most transient emotion of the mind, could come into existence without a cause, it is evident that the whole universe and all the inhabitants it contains might also exist without a cause..."*

Aunt March pulls her gaze from the window. "Why did you stop?"

I look at her, then the page. "I don't... I don't agree with what Belsham says."

She rolls her eyes and folds her hands in her lap with an air of patience—when she truly lacks any at all. "Do tell me why."

"Because I wouldn't want my worth to be diminished if someone else doesn't live up to *their* expectations."

"Josyphine, *you're* not living up to your expectations," Aunt March reminds me with lifted brows. "You're flighty and awkward and you think too much and, God, don't get me started on the writing."

Butterflies shimmy up my center. Rather than anger or irritation plaguing me, insecurity takes my heart. I heave a sigh and run my fingers along the page. "You'll regret that when I'm a famous author one day."

Remorse shadows her as she sits up, clenches her jaw, and clears her throat. She may be poky most of the time, but my great-Aunt March has a heart buried beneath her judgmental remarks. "I'll deal with that issue when I get there," she says. "Now, that's not what Belsham is saying."

"Yes, it is."

"No, you indolent child," she blurts. "He's saying that you must have a reason for living or else your life is for nothing."

I hum and let my eyes wander the polished study in thought. The shelves are immaculately dusted with plenty of old books that could occupy one for hours. If Belsham is saying there must be a reason or cause, then, "What must the reason look like?"

"What do you mean?"

"Does the cause for living have to be about having money, or can it be simple like reading books or,"—Aunt March's pet parrot squawks on her perch—"caring for animals."

Aunt March mulls over the words in silent moments. "A good question, Josyphine." She sucks her teeth and gazes out of the window. Then her voice quiets to a murmur. "A good question."

CHAPTER 7

BUDDING FRIENDSHIPS

One snowy afternoon, I trudge outside with a shovel. Last night, Marmee gave us another story about being grateful for what we have, so I begin shoveling the garden walkway for no benefit of my own. No flowers bloom in the height of winter, but Beth loves to take walks when the sun shines bright.

My gaze travels to the mansion across the way. It looks much different from my shabby home, but mine fills with love and joy. The mansion appears lifeless. No children frolic about and no motherly face smiles through the windows. The other day, I spotted Laurie's longing expression staring through the window at Amy and Beth having a snowball fight.

Wealth doesn't equal happiness.

Keeping this in mind, I store away the shovel and tromp over to the big house. At the lonely corner where the sad boy sits, I launch a snowball at the window. The *thud* startles him.

"How are you?" I ask when he opens the window. "Are you sick?"

"I was," he croaks. "I've had a bad cold. Been shut up for a week."

I frown. "Aw. What do you amuse yourself with?"

Laurie shakes his head. "Nothing. It's dull as tombs up here."

"Don't you read?"

"Not much. They won't let me."

"Can someone read to you?"

"Grandpa does sometimes, but my books don't interest him and I hate asking Brooke all the time."

I huff and gaze across the field at my house. I fear I made Laurie uncomfortable last time I tried to push my way into his life—when I made declarations that he would teach me French and tell me stories. But if he *invites* me...

"Have someone come see you, then."

He shrugs. "There isn't anyone I'd like to see. Boys make such a row and my head is weak."

He's not making this easy. I curl my mittened fingers into fists and ask, "Isn't there some nice girl who'd read and amuse you?"

He tilts his head in consideration, then says, "Don't know any."

I groan and throw my hands in the air. By Jove, boys are more clueless than I imagined! "Theodore Laurence!" I point to my face. "Hel-*lo!*"

Laurie startles, his face lighting up as he leans out the window. "Oh—you! Will you come? Please do!"

"I'll ask Mother," I say with a grin. "Shut the window like a good boy and wait for me." Once I march home and ask Marmee, my sisters fly about in attempts to hand over gifts to help him feel better.

"You can't go with your hair like that!" Meg says, trying to wrench my hair into a bun.

I shake her off. "Yes I can, and I will!"

"At least a braid," she begs.

Before I can protest, she removes my newsboy hat and begins to braid in a fluid motion. The moment she finishes, I gather all the goodies—and Beth's kittens—in my arms and dart back over to the house. But as I walk up the steps, I find myself wanting to ensure no hair sticks in my face nor pokes out in odd places. The attempt makes the kittens fussy, so I push the desire aside and step into the house when a servant opens the door.

All thoughts of vanity disappear as the grand foyer steals my breath. The ceiling stretches up high with a glimmering chandelier in the center. And I thought Aunt March's house was the fanciest I've ever seen.

"Is it up to your standards?" Laurie says suddenly.

I flinch from my reverie and grin. "It's—magnificent." Then I rush forward and hand him the kittens. "Beth thought her cats would be comforting. Don't laugh—oh, I knew you would! I couldn't refuse. She was so anxious to do something helpful. Mother sends her love and Meg wanted me to bring some of her blancmange. She's not a bad cook, it turns out."

Laurie giggles and cradles the kittens. "Thank you. Consider me comforted." When I uncover the dish, his eyes widen. "That looks far too pretty to eat."

A servant removes the dish from my hands and takes it to the kitchen. We head into the parlor and I gape once more at the bookshelves—in the *parlor!* "*Whoa,*" I whisper. "What a cozy room this is!"

Laurie sits on a tufted sofa and places the kitchens on the cushion. "It might be if it was kept nice, but the maids are lazy. I don't know how to make them mind."

I quirk my lips to one side as I study the room. In a swift movement, I remove my cloak and fling it onto a reading chair. I'm wearing a plaid skirt, a blouse, a vest, and a loosely tied cravat. I slip off my hat and flap my hands on my head to keep the frizz at bay.

"I can right it up in two minutes!" I say, jumping right to work. "Only the hearth must be brushed. And—the things made straight on the mantelpiece." I speak distractedly as I organize and bustle about. "And the books put here—and there. The bottles will go here... Up," I demand, shooing him and the kittens from the sofa. "It must be turned from the light. And—the pillows plumped a bit." I stand in the center of the room and plant my hands on my hips with a satisfied huff. "Now then. All good."

"How kind you are!" Laurie exclaims as he plops back on the sofa. "Take the big chair, please. Allow me to amuse my company."

I lower into the reading chair, but I protest, "No, I came to amuse you." Planting my chin on the back of the chair, I stare at the bookshelf with big eyes. "Shall I read aloud?"

"Oh, I've read all those. If you don't mind, I'd rather talk."

I whirl around and recline, throwing my legs over one of the arms. "Not a bit! I'll talk all day if you get me going. Beth says I never know when to stop."

Laurie turns toward me, petting one of the kittens. "Is Beth the rosy one who stays home a good deal and always walks with a basket?"

"Yes, that's my girl."

"So," he begins, squinting in thought, "the pretty one is Meg. And Amy is the one with light hair, right?"

My head lolls as I look at him with a smile creeping up. "All correct. Which one does that make me?"

Color rushes to Laurie's face. He allows soft kitten fur to distract him. When he finally looks up, he says, "The soulful one... When I look over to your house, you all seem to be up to good times. I don't mean to be rude and stare, but it gets lonely up here. And you... you seem like the spark of your family. They wouldn't shine as bright without you."

Color rushes to my face as well. The affirmation sails straight to my warm heart, especially when Aunt March's declarations of my failures continue to hover over my spirit. I clear my throat. "You won't be lonely anymore. You have us. Do you think your grandpa would let you come over a lot?"

"I think so—if your mother asks him. He might look mean, but I assure you he's not. He lets me do as I like. He'll be afraid I might be a bother to strangers."

"We're not strangers, we're neighbors! You'd never be a bother, Teddy."

We fall into conversation about random things and moments that made us laugh in the past. At the memory of Aunt March's parrot swiping the wig of the old gentleman who'd come to woo her, we laugh so hard that my stomach cramps and my eyes water. I confess my plans and hopes about the future—that I will one day be the world's greatest authoress. Upon this revelation, Laurie says that he loves reading as much as I do, but he has read even more books than I because of how many his grandfather owns.

"You mean you own more books than what's in this room?" I cry, jumping up. "Oh, you must show me at once!"

Laurie grins and leaps up, grabbing my wrist. We dash out of the parlor and through the hallways. I can't help stumbling to a stop at the sight of the grand rooms and wonderfully decorated walls.

He waits for me as I wander through the various drawing rooms, tea rooms, parlors, and studies. By Jove, how many rooms does one house need? There's a clear spot between two bookshelves that can hide me with ease. I slip into it when he calls, "Jo, where'd you go?"

I press my fingers to my lips to keep from laughing.

"Jo," Laurie sings. "Are you hiding?"

His footsteps close in and I leap and shout, "*BOO!*" I cackle when his shoulders tense and he gasps.

"Jo—!"

"Try to keep up!" I call and dash out of the study into the hallway. There is so much room to prance about and chase; it's hard not to take advantage of it.

I frolic through the hallway past many rooms. Suddenly, Laurie yells, "Think fast!" as he lurches from my right and grabs my wrists. I yelp as he swings me into another room. What I don't know is that this room has a few stairs leading down into it. I trip over the steps and fall to the ground, taking him with me.

Our laughing echoes through the room as he lands on top of me. The air jumps out of my lungs as his chest presses against mine.

"You cheated." I giggle as he rolls aside, both of us fighting to catch our breaths.

"That wasn't a real game!" he protests.

"Yeah, yeah." I brush stray curls from my face as I rise to my feet. A gasp escapes me. "Is this the library?"

Laurie situates himself. "It is. Grandfather is out, so you needn't be afraid."

I toss a glare at him. "Pfft. I'm not afraid of anything."

"I don't believe you are," he replies in a gentle tone, admiration glimmering in his black eyes.

I turn away before he can see my blush and wander around the library, my hands clasped together. The tall windows allow the afternoon sun to brighten the walls lined with books. There are portraits and statues and darling little glass cabinets filled with trinkets. Dazzling Sleepy Hollow chairs catch my eye. The room has handsome tables and bronzes and a lovely fireplace I can sit in front of all day and never grow tired. I could live my entire life in this room and be content!

"What richness," I whisper and collapse into a velour chair.

"Theodore Laurence, you ought to be the happiest boy in the world."

Laurie shakes his head and perches on a table. "A fellow can't live on books."

My gaze savors the bookshelves. "Only if you read the wrong stories."

Chapter 8

Fear And Compliments

When Laurie asks whether I mind he sees the doctor for a moment, I lurch to my feet and reply, "Don't mind me. I'm happy as a cricket here," as I scour the shelves.

He flees the room and I wander before a portrait of old Mr. Laurence—pale skin and bald head and bushy white beard. "Meh," I wonder aloud, "I'm not afraid of you." My fingers hover above the painted face. "You've got such kind eyes, though you look like you have a tremendous will of your own. You aren't as handsome as *my* grandfather... but I like you."

"Thank you, ma'am," a gruff voice says. My heart leaps into my throat as I whirl around to see the subject of the painting standing in the doorway. For a quick moment, I consider the consequences if I were to dash out of the room, but he's standing at the only exit. "So you're not afraid of me, eh?" Mr. Laurence says, hobbling deeper into the library.

I pull myself to my full height and lift my chin. "No, sir."

"And you don't think I'm as handsome as your grandfather?"

"No, sir."

"And I've got a tremendous will, have I?"

"I only said I thought so." I knot my hands behind my back, then add, "Sir."

He quirks a bushy brow. "But you like me in spite of it?"

I nod once. "Yes, sir."

After a pause, Mr. Laurence gives a short laugh. He walks closer and sets his finger under my chin. His grave eyes study me as he tilts my head side to side. It feels insulting to be examined in such a way. I remove my head from his grasp and step back.

"What have you been trying to do with this boy of mine?" he asks. His sharp tone tightens my chest; I brush it off because he's a mere mortal man and no one to fear.

"I'm only being neighborly."

His gaze narrows. "You think he needs a bit of cheering up, do you?"

I clear my throat of nerves. "Yes, he seems lonely. And we only would like to help if we can, for we want to thank you for the Christmas present you sent us."

The hesitation begins to slip from his demeanor. A subtle smile tugs at the lips hidden beneath the beard. "That was all the boy. How is the poor woman you helped?"

"Better, sir!" Eager to keep the old man's lighter spirits, I ramble on about the Hummels and the kids and what kind of conditions they live in and how I was happy to give everything I had because I'm lucky enough to have a warm fire every day. In the midst of my rambling, a bell rings.

"That's the tea bell," Mr. Laurence says. "Would you like to join my grandson and me?"

Very few old people like or even tolerate me; Mr. Laurence's hospitality and kindness lift my mood and draw a grin on my face. "I would love to," I reply, trying to smother my eagerness with an even tone. "Thank you."

He offers his arm to me in such an old-fashioned manner. For the afternoon, I speak with Laurie and Mr. Laurence and they try to convince me to play the piano, which I refuse, for I would surely break it without even trying. When Laurie plays, a reprehensible expression paints his grandfather's face and I cannot get the sight out of my mind for the rest of the day.

Before I can slip out and venture home, Laurie tells me there's one last thing he wants to show me—the conservatory. The flickering lights dance upon the colorful flowers. I press my nose into one of them and inhale.

"I had it lighted just for you," Laurie says. Instead of replying, the pollen makes me sneeze once, twice, three times. It sends both of us into a fit of laughter. The conservatory is from a fairytale; both sides are covered in green and the vines dangling over the walkways create a tunnel.

"Meg would love this," I mutter. "She loves flowers and pretty things."

My fingers brush over the colorful petals and leaves. The damp air hums around me and I can feel my hair growing more and more frizzy. I close my eyes and imagine the vines reaching out to wrap around my arm, growing into my body. What if I became part plant? I stand in the conservatory with vines embedded in my skin. I wield it like a lasso, throwing a vine to a pipe on the ceiling and pulling myself up. With a flick and draw of my arm, I create a swing and dangle above Laurie. He looks up at me with a grin. I wiggle my fingers and a flurry of blue flower petals rain down on him. His laughter echoes.

Laurie clears his throat to yank me from my daydream. I turn around to see him with an armful of cut flowers—begonias and daisies and marigolds and roses. The hues blend in such a beautiful manner it saddens me that they'll die soon. Suddenly, the bouquet isn't as charming as it should be.

"Please give these to your mother for me," he says, slipping the bouquet into my arms with a soulful look. "And thank her for the medicine she sent."

And with a smile and cradle of the flowers, I bid him farewell and trample home. Later that night, when Meg is combing my freshly washed hair for me, I blurt, "Marmee, why doesn't Mr. Laurence like to let Laurie play piano?"

Marmee combs Beth's wet hair and Beth combs Amy's wet hair, for wash days in the March household are a laborious affair and none of us ever feels like doing our own.

"I'm not exactly sure, but I think it's because his daughter, Laurie's mother, ran off to Italy and married a man from Malaya. The gentleman was lovely and accomplished, but Mr. Laurence still didn't like him because he rarely saw his daughter afterward. They both died when Laurie was small and Mr. Laurence took him in. Laurie comes naturally by his love of music, for he is like his mother, and I dare say his grandfather fears that he may want to be a musician and run off like her. At any rate, his skill reminds him of the man he did not like."

"That's romantic," Meg muses.

"That's ridiculous!" I scowl. "Let him be a musician if he wants and not plague his life."

"That's why he has such handsome black eyes and pretty manners."

"What would you know about his eyes and manners!" I bite fiercely. "You've barely spoken to him." A tightness in my gut flares. I grow more frustrated, hating the feeling.

"I met him at the party and what you told me says he knows how to behave. A kind little gentleman living in the Mansion of Bliss." She sighs. "That was a cute little speech about the medicine Mother sent him. And sending the flowers too. Adorable."

"For Marmee and the blancmange, I suppose," I grumble.

Meg laughs. "Oh, come on, Jo. Don't be stupid. They were for you."

My eyes widen. "For *me*? Whatever for?"

My older sister laughs louder. "Oh, you don't know a compliment when you get one."

I scoff and lean against her knee as she continues detangling my hair. "Don't spoil my fun. Laurie's a nice boy and I like him a lot. I won't have any romantic stuff ruining it. Besides, flowers as a compliment are silly. We'll all be good to him because he hasn't got a mother. And he'll come over and see us, right, Marmee?"

"Yes, Jo," Marmee says and begins to run some oil through Beth's hair. "Your little friend is very welcome." Then she throws a pointed look at Meg. "And I hope Meg will remember that children should be children as long as they can."

FRUSTRATION WEAVES THROUGH MY FAMILY OVER THE SPAN of a week.

One day, Beth accompanies me to the Laurence mansion. She begins to bloom as she swallows the sight of such a grand home, nearly blossoming entirely when seeing the Laurences' piano. While I know of Mr. Laurence's predisposition against piano playing, I don't have the heart to stop her as the light glimmers in her eyes. But, Mr. Laurence, startled and grumpy, snaps at my sister. Now poor Beth vows to never leave our house again.

Another morning, before Meg and I drop Amy off at school, she calls Laurie a regular cyclops when he passes us on horseback! I grow defensive rather quickly and call my boy's eyes quite handsome, and soon realize Amy meant centaur. While I laugh at her blunder, an uneasiness trembles through my body, for I was so quick to call Laurie handsome.

Nonetheless, my frustration with myself vanishes when

Amy arrives home crying later that afternoon. Her teacher, Mr. Davis, thrashed her hand over pickled limes! I don't believe I've ever heard something so ludicrous.

The entire family flies about the house, trying to discover the proper way to handle Mr. Davis's petty deed. Marmee sends me a warning glare every time I suggest we tie him up and give him a taste of his own medicine.

"Josephine, we don't tolerate violence in this family," she lectures. "I shouldn't have to remind you of that."

Beth, who thinks her kittens will heal broken spirits every time, doesn't let Amy spend two minutes without cradling one to her chest. As I debate with Meg about my idea of justice, Marmee buts in.

"Jo, dear, Laurie is waving out the window. Do go outside and talk to him. Fresh air will do you some good."

I storm outside and meet Laurie in the garden. I'm not wearing my cloak, but my Sontag shawl is enough to keep me warm because my anger heats me a great deal.

"What's going on?"

"Mr. Davis thrashed Amy's hand for bringing pickled limes to school."

His jaw drops. "How cruel! How would he like it if someone did that to him?"

I stomp my foot. "That's what I said! Marmee says she *did* break the rules, but she doesn't agree with the punishment. Amy will be staying home from now on before Mother decides what to do with her. Ugh—what is it with old men taking their anger out on little girls?"

Laurie stands straight and protests, "Now, my grandfather is trying to mend snapping at poor Beth. He just—"

"Oh, I know, Teddy," I break in, planting a hand on my hip and patting his arm with the other. "That wasn't fair of me. I apologize, dear boy. I don't want to see my sisters upset. Papa made me the man of the house while he's gone and I feel as if I failed to protect them."

"That's not true," Laurie says, slinging an arm across my shoulders and dragging me toward the house. "You protect them with all your might and anyone should be lucky to have a strong sister like you. You might make a reckless mother, but you make a strong father."

I wrap my arm around his waist. "I can't tell if you're complimenting me."

He considers for a moment as we walk. "Me neither."

"In any case, thank you, my boy," I say with a laugh. "Let's play a game of chess to distract me."

"You're horrible at chess."

"I make my own rules."

Inside, everyone is still flying about, but calm a little at the sight of Laurie. We flop on the ground and begin playing. Marmee tells Amy in a soft voice, "You must study a little every day with Beth, okay? I don't approve of corporal punishment, especially for girls. I—"

"We are not fragile beings, Mother," I defend as I knock away one of Laurie's knights with my own.

He protests. "You can't—"

"Shh," I hiss, then look at Marmee. "It is little children who can't handle thrashing, not capable teens. Girls are as strong as boys."

"Not now, Jo," Meg says.

I lean toward her while propped on my elbows. "If not now, when?"

Marmee sighs and turns to Amy. I miss whatever she says to her, for I notice—

"You cheater!"

Laurie's eyes glimmer with innocence, but I see right through it.

"That's not where my queen was!"

"Yes, it was."

"Liar." I know he's lying because he doesn't protest when I move it back to the place I remember it.

I snort when I hear Marmee say, "You are getting to be rather conceited, my dear, and it's time you set about correcting it. You have a good many little gifts and virtues, but there's no need for parading them. Remember, the greatest charm of all is modesty."

"So it is!" Laurie agrees and steals yet another of my knights.

"You can't do that—"

"Quiet now, Jo." He looks at Marmee. "I knew a girl, once. She had a remarkable talent for music and didn't know it. She never would have guessed how amazing her composing was, not even if anyone told her."

Beth, curled on the couch, says, "I wish I'd known her. Maybe she would have helped me. I'm so stupid."

I frown. "Bethy, don't say that."

"You *do* know her," Laurie says with a suggestive hint in his eyes. Beth reddens and takes my favorite pillow and buries her face in it.

When he catches my gaze, I smile. It warms my heart how he praises Beth in any situation he can. His recent induction into this family teaches me that, despite the rampant fears in the world, a compliment can mend an aching heart.

CHAPTER 9

UP IN FLAMES

Later that evening, Beth is playing the piano, Meg is off sewing in the bedroom, Amy is elsewhere, and Laurie and I curl up on the couch, gossiping about the play he invited Meg and me to tomorrow.

"No, no, you'll just have to rewrite it," Laurie says.

I elbow him, my folded knees falling across his lap. "I can't *steal* an idea. I have morals."

He arches a brow at me. "Truly, Jo, dear?"

I scrunch my face and flick his nose. "This isn't about me and my morals—or lack of."

He brushes a finger across his nose and ruffles his hair. "I'll be sure to tell Ned and Samuel to be on their best behavior."

"They're boys," I scoff. "I'm not hopeful."

He feigns hurt with a hand to his chest. "I'm a boy."

"You're a *special* boy. You're Teddy. I wouldn't dare to hold any of your rich friends to the same expectation I hold you to."

"I suppose you won't be Mrs. Ned Moffat anytime soon, then."

I grimace. What a horrid thought! "Please don't say such things, Teddy. Let's just hope *The Seven Castles* ought to be good enough. By Jove—can you imagine owning seven castles? Well—of course *you* can. You've got a castle of your own!"

He wraps his arms around my legs and leans his head against my knees. The blazing fireplace illuminates his face. "That's not true. I do wish you wouldn't always speak of my money. It's not part of who I am."

"It's easy to ignore it when you have it. It's the reason we have wonderful seats at the *theater*," I cry in a hushed tone as giddiness shudders down my spine.

"We'll have a capital time. We—"

The moving figure in the corner of my eye makes me pat his curly head. "Shh, shh," I say as Amy walks into the room. She'll have a bratty meltdown if she finds out she's not invited.

"What are you talking about?" she asks, dropping in front of the fireplace to warm her hands.

"None of your business," I snap.

Before Amy can start her tantrum, Laurie gets to his feet and sings, "Okay, it's time for me to go. I'll see you later."

Amy scowls.

THE SECRET IS NO USE; AMY BOUNCES INTO THE BEDROOM the next day and plops onto her bed.

"Where are you going?" she asks.

I situate the outfit I'd worn to the Gardiner's New Year's Eve party and try to fix my bun, which lacks all elegance. My frustration with my unattractive hair and nagging sister causes my temper to seize my chest with a fiery fist. "Little children shouldn't poke where they're not wanted."

"Do tell me!" she insists, turning toward Meg, who sits on our bed lacing up her shoes. "I should think you'd let me go, too.

Beth is fussing over her piano and I haven't got anything to do. I'm lonely!"

"I can't," Meg says with a sorrowful expression. "You're not invited."

Marmee said that Amy is growing too conceited, so she must learn that she doesn't have to be the star of everything. "You can't go," I add, glaring at her through the mirror. "So don't be a baby and whine about it."

"You're going somewhere with Laurie, I know you are! You were whispering about it on the sofa last night! Aren't you going with him?"

"Yes, now be still and stop talking."

As I gather my shawl, Amy bursts, "The theater!" Then she gasps, her bright eyes wide. "You're going to see *The Seven Castles!* Oh, I *shall* go. Mother said I might see it and I've got money!"

Meg tries to soothe our littlest sister by promising she'll see the play with Hannah and Beth, but that's not good enough for the conceited brat.

"No, I'd rather go with you and Laurie! Oh, please let me go! Please, please!"

I turn around to see Meg's questioning gaze. She raises a brow and lifts her shoulder.

"*No,*" I say. "If she goes, I won't, and Laurie won't like that and it'll be very rude since he only invited us. And we drag in Amy?" My gaze slides to her. This is a valuable lesson she should learn. "I would think she'd hate to poke herself in places she isn't wanted."

Amy stomps toward her trunk and begins to slip on her boots. "I shall go if Meg says I can and I'll pay for myself. Laurie has nothing to do with it."

"Our seats are reserved so you can't sit with us and you can't sit alone so Teddy will give up his seat and that will spoil everything. Or he'll get you another seat which is improper and rude when you *weren't asked!* Sit still and shut up!"

With one boot on, Amy starts crying and Laurie calls from downstairs. I scoff and pull a despondent Meg into the hallway.

"Since when did you start calling him Teddy?" she asks as we trample down the stairs.

My face warms. "Hush."

"You'll pay for this!" Amy yells.

Before I slam the door behind me, I shout back, *"Fiddlesticks!"*

I push the thought of Amy to the back of my mind as Meg and I loop our arms through Laurie's. Two of his friends and Mr. Brooke accompany us, but they don't pay much attention to Meg and me. The theater is such a grand building with gilded designs and carvings decorating everywhere my gaze lands. I haven't even seen the play yet and I'm impressed. I wish I could run my fingers over the golden carvings. I can dig up stories hidden in the curves and grooves.

"I knew you'd like it," Laurie mutters.

I turn toward him, his black eyes glimmering as he looks at me. A blush runs up my neck. My arm tightens around his and I press my cheek to his shoulder for a moment. With a big family like mine, I've never been able to be me and *only* me. I've always been Josephine March—sister of Amy, Meg, and Beth. Never Jo March, writer of phenomenal stories. The love and affection I've received have been a dished-out serving, for my sisters need some too. It's all the same, tailored ever so slightly for each of us.

But being friends with Teddy... it's the first time someone is thinking of me—and only me.

The theater invitation is almost enough for me to feel every bit of my authentic self—but I cannot shake the guilt. Amy wanted to come so badly and I was so harsh. I was trying to teach her manners because it is improper to invite yourself places. But in turn, I forgot my own. It's easy to lose the little amount of hold I have on my temper when it comes to my sisters.

I don't want to admit I'm jealous of Amy; she's got plenty of dreadful flaws. Perhaps some of our quarrels are because of my inability to accept that she has a better childhood than I did. Poverty forced Marmee to work more often than not, leaving Meg and me to look after Beth and Amy. When times were rougher than usual, Meg and I would take turns spending weeks at Aunt and Uncle March's house so Marmee and Papa didn't fret over another mouth to feed. Feeling as though you're a burden to your own family is the most horrid experience of mine.

Amy knows none of this struggle and whines like her life is the worst in the world! The most irritating part is that it works so dreadfully well. The world takes pity on the suffering Amy March—and scolds me for not acting more like her.

It felt good being considered first, and I will carry that feeling close, but I also have a sisterly duty to teach wrong from right in proper ways—and I failed. I try with such strength to tame my temper; I fail most of the time. When anger flares in my chest, I must get it out lest it burns me alive. In turn, it burns other people. People I care about—like Amy.

Despite the sparkling elves and princes and princesses, I can't enjoy the play the way I want to. Also because Laurie's rowdy friends are often hushed by other guests. It takes all of my strength not to run home and apologize to my sister.

"Teddy," I say once the play is over and we walk into the lobby. "I don't have any money with me. I was wickedly cruel to Amy before the play and I feel terrible. I want to buy her chocolate from the concession stand. I'll pay you back the moment we return." With a gentle smile, Laurie pats my hand and walks toward the concession stand.

Meg touches my shoulder. "I'm proud of you."

"I was trying to teach her."

She nods. "I know."

Off to the side, one of Laurie's friends—Ned—makes obscene gestures and poses with a statue. An employee reprimands him and Meg and I turn away, lest we be seen as part of his group.

"Must his friends be so abominable?" Meg asks, earning a snort from me.

At home, Amy reads in the parlor and never lifts her eyes from the book. Neither of us would have spoken about the play if Beth hadn't asked. Meg relays the night's events and I dart upstairs for the money to pay back Laurie. I half expect my top drawer to be overturned or my clothes to be strewn everywhere. But everything is in its place. Even my money.

I retrieve and give it to Laurie. Once he departs, I lower beside Amy.

"I feel bad for being mean," I say, toying with the box of chocolate. "Here, as—as a peace offering."

Amy hesitates, eyeing the box. She's the only person I know whose affection can be bought, despite Marmee saying it can't be. Without a word, she snatches the box and opens them.

She's still twelve, I remind myself. *It'll all be over in the morning.*

I wake before everyone else the next morning and slip into the attic to work. For an hour and a half, I write various short stories inspired by the carvings I saw at the theater. I slide open the drawer to work on my novel, but—it's not where I last put it. And, despite spending the next ten minutes rifling through the attic, it's not here. Not even scraps to prove Scrabble chewed it up.

I rush downstairs into the parlor, breathless and frantic. "Has anyone seen my book?"

"No," Beth and Meg say, exchanging confused and worried glances. But Amy pokes the fire silently.

"Amy," I warn.

After a moment, she looks up at me and shrugs with a superior air. "I haven't got it."

Anxiety rumbles in my gut. "Then you know where it is."

Amy sniffs. "No, I don't."

"That's a lie!" I shout, yanking her from the fireplace and standing over her. She leans on her elbows and looks at me with fear in her eyes.

"It isn't," she says defiantly. "I don't got it, and I don't know where it is, and I don't care!"

I bend my knees and lean closer to her face, my hair dangling over my shoulders. "You know something, and you better tell me or I'll make you!" My voice booms through the house with such fear and anger I've never felt before. My chest feels like it's going to explode.

"Jo," Meg warns.

A wicked little smile tugs at her lips as she crawls backward and rises to her feet. "Doesn't matter what you do, you'll never see your stupid little book again!"

"Why—why not?"

She lifts her chin. "I burned it up."

I gasp, my hands flying to my mouth as tears fill my eyes at the mere suggestion of it, whether it's true or not. "What—are— did you really?"

"Yes, I did!" Amy exclaims.

My book. My precious book—the one I spent hours on, enduring aching hands and an aching back and tired eyes.

"I told you I'd make you pay for being so cross yesterday."

"Amy," Meg whispers in disbelief.

"Did you truly?" asks Beth.

My biggest contribution to this family. The piece of work

that makes me feel like I deserve a place in this world—and it's nothing but a pile of ashes now. Belsham wrote that whatever begins to exist must have an adequate cause for its existence. And Amy stole my cause, my reason for living. It's as if she killed me.

"And I—"

I don't let Amy finish. The flare of anger in my chest takes over and I grab her arm with one hand and her hair with the other and throw her to the ground as hard as I can.

"Jo, stop!" Meg yells.

I poured my best ideas into that book—and they're gone forever. "*I HATE YOU!*" I scream, landing on top of Amy and smacking away her defensive hands, grabbing her by the throat. "I HATE YOU SO MUCH! I CAN NEVER WRITE IT AGAIN BECAUSE OF YOU!"

Hot tears stream down my face. Everything is closing in on me. My book, my characters—*they're all gone*. It feels like Amy reached her hand into my chest and ripped out my heart.

Amy shrieks and Meg pries my fingers from our youngest sister's throat as Beth pulls me back. Before Beth wraps her arms around mine to trap them against my body, I lash out and my nails rake across Amy's face. Beth and Meg are trying to calm the situation, but nothing will ever put out this fire. I never imagined Amy would ruin something so important to me.

"I HATE YOU! I'LL NEVER FORGIVE YOU!"

I shake off Beth and run up into the attic. There's no point in writing anything anymore. I bury my face in the sofa and mourn the loss of the most important piece of work I've ever created. Soon, Meg and Beth come upstairs and comfort me in silence.

"I-I-I—I'm nothing without my—without my book," I sob. "It's my—my life!"

It will take me years before I complete something of that

quality again. I'd spent the last two years on that book, and the reminder of all that wasted dedication makes me sob more.

"Jo," Marmee says, her voice startling me.

I look up from Beth's lap, my head pounding, to see Mother and Amy standing at the top of the staircase. Amy's eyes are red.

"I'm so sorry, Jo. Please forgive me."

"You're just sorry no one's doting on you anymore!" I seethe. "I will *never* forgive you for such a thing as long as I live."

As the days pass, nothing pacifies me.

I am still as hurt as the moment I found out. Marmee tries to talk me down and encourage me to forgive. Yet I follow the advice she's always given me: *follow your heart.* My heart is too sore to let Amy back in and shows no sign of recovery so far.

Since losing my manuscript, Marmee and Meg have to refrain me from burning the rest of my work. Meg goes as far as confiscating my bundle of short stories to protect them.

"You'll thank me later," she says before kissing my tear-stained cheek.

One evening, while we all knit in silence, I allow the bubbling ideas to flood through my mind again. Hopelessness has been flooding me, but the new story ideas keep knocking on my brain's door.

"I find it ironic," Amy says to break the quiet, "that people who always talk about being good don't even try when other people set them a virtuous example."

Yesterday, she adopted her bratty air again, having lifted her nose and declaring that she'd "done her part" and "it's time I do mine" so I could move on. I *can* move on, but she won't be with me when I do it.

No one replies, not even Marmee, but I can feel her gaze on me.

"Shut up, Amy," I say, getting to my feet and venturing into the attic.

The road to forgiveness can be considered if writing isn't ruined for me forever.

Chapter 10

Down In Water

My anger has begun to subside, but my hurt hasn't.

One morning, Laurie skips into the house to take me skating for the last ice of the season. I'd promised to take Amy, but I leave her calling for me and dash toward the lake with my skates. With the sun against the snow blinding us, Laurie and I throw snowballs at one another. I howl with laughter when my snowball hits him square in the face. He pulls me toward the frozen lake.

Behind us, Amy shouts to wait for her.

I push forward when I sense Laurie's hesitance.

"Jo—"

"No," I insist.

"But—"

I whip toward him. "Whose side are you on?"

Laurie tosses a glance at Amy, then at me. He throws an arm across my shoulders. "Yours, of course. Come on."

He let me roam his home library for hours after finding out what she'd done. *"Read,"* he told me, *"so you can get inspiration to write another book. You can do it. I know you can."*

"You look like a Russian," I tease, brushing my gloved hand over his fur-trimmed hat.

He shrugs with a smirk. "Maybe I am—secretly."

We tie on our skates and step onto the ice. I'm horrible at skating, but a few times I can soar without fail. Yet Laurie usually bumps his hip against mine to make me tumble onto the ice.

Both laughing, he reaches toward me. I stare at him with a scrunched nose. Instead of letting him help me up, I snatch his hand and pull him down with me.

"*Oof—*"

He lands across my lap and my laughter fills my chest with crisp air.

"Now we're square," I say with a smug expression as I push him off.

"Fair enough, I suppose." He reaches up and honks my nose. We help each other to our feet, cautious of whether one of us will break the truce and shove someone. A moment of silence passes between us as our gazes stay locked with our faces on the verge of laughing.

Laurie slowly backs up, fixes his ridiculous hat, and skates on. "Stay away from the middle!"

"Got it!" I dust myself off and begin to trail behind him until hearing a crackling echo, followed by a splash and a yelp.

"Jo—!"

Chills shudder through my body as I whirl around and see my littlest sister's head disappear under the lake. My heart seizes.

"AMY!"

The scream rips from my throat, thick with terror and raspy with sorrow. Numbness vibrates down my body as I skate toward her as fast as I can, yelling her name over and over.

"Jo, no!" I hear Laurie shout. He takes my arm and yanks me back. "You can't—it'll break and take you under too!"

The jolt stops me and I fall onto the ice, my entire body frozen.

Amy, Amy, Amy.

Her honey-blond curls and her desperate attempts to be the best she can be.

She's just a child—turning thirteen in a month.

Amy, Amy, Amy.

She had burned my book into nothing and I hate her for it, but I love her for so much more. I write for my family. I *write* for Amy—without Amy, there's no me.

"JO!"

Laurie's voice sends a shock through me. He's dragging her out of the river with a branch by the time I snap back into reality. She's dripping and coughing and crying and he pulls her to the side and I finally skate over, my bones ringing and trembling.

I untie my cape and wrap it around her then peel off her gloves and replace them with my own. I rip off Laurie's hat and place it on her head.

"I'm sorry," Amy wails, her head in my lap. "I'm sorry. I'm so sorry, Jo."

I hush and press a kiss to her forehead. It isn't until Laurie and I are void of our cold-weather gear do we bring her home. I can't hear anything they're saying. I don't listen. I focus on the sight of my baby sister moving, living, breathing. Even if she's crying—that means she's alive.

The next hour passes in a blur. My mind spins as I fly about the house, one shoe on and one shoe off, my hands cut and bleeding from the ice, disregarding any concern about myself until Amy is fast asleep, rolled in blankets in front of a blazing fire.

"Let me clean your cuts," Marmee says in a quiet tone. She lowers beside me as I watch Amy sleep.

"Are you sure she's safe?"

"Quite safe, dear. She's not hurt and will likely not even suffer a cold." She tilts her head toward me to catch my eyes. "Because you were sensible enough to cover her and get her home so quickly."

Tears sting my eyes. "Laurie did it all. I-I—I froze, Marmee. As Amy was drowning, I froze." I inhale. "I didn't move until she was out of the water. If she died, it would have been my fault." I press my knees against my chest and lower my head to hide the tears I can't fight anymore. "It's my dreadful temper," I sob. "I-I try—so hard to stop it, and then it breaks out worse." Marmee wraps her arm around me and I collapse into her chest. "Oh, Mother, what do I do?"

She brushes the stray hair from my face and kisses my temple. "Observe and hope, my love. Never get tired of trying. You can conquer your faults."

"You don't understand how bad it is. When—when I get like this, it's like—I have no remorse or care about who I hurt. I could hurt someone—and *like* it. All because they wronged me in the slightest way. One day, I'll do something unforgivable and everyone will hate me. I don't want that to happen, Marmee. *Please* tell me what to do."

I hide my face in her arm as if hiding from the humiliating confession. No matter how much I call Amy a conceited brat, I'm a hotheaded brute. I'll stir trouble for trouble's sake.

"I'll help you, my child. Don't cry so. Just remember today and resolve with all your soul that you will never see such a day again. We all have our temptations. Some far greater than yours. Sometimes, it takes us all our lives to conquer our faults. You think your temper is the worst in the world, that I may not understand, but mine used to be just like it."

Her words make me sit up. I stare at her through my blurry eyes and wipe away a tear. "Truly? Why, you're never angry!"

Marmee brushes a thumb over my cheek. "I am angry nearly every day of my life. I've been curing it for forty years. And sometimes, my method of cure doesn't work. I've learned not to show it and I still want to learn not to feel it. It may take me another forty years to do so, but that's life. It's better I keep trying to tame it, for the journey of bettering oneself is superior to a journey of letting anger roam free."

Her shameless confession comforts me. Even after I hit Amy or after I say something cruel—to whoever—my mother never shows anger toward me. It's as though she's above the emotion. As though she's mastered every foul thing in the world. As I watch her now, her many dreadlocks weaved into two French braids that twirl into a bun at her nape, I dig up certain memories. "Are—are you angry when you tense your lips tight and leave the room sometimes—like when Aunt March scolds or people worry you?"

Marmee gives me a gentle smile and takes my hand. "Yes, I've learned to stop the hasty words that threaten me. When I feel intense enough to break through that barrier, I leave the room for a minute to shake myself out of it. My unleashed anger will hurt the situation rather than help it."

"How do you learn to keep still?" I cross my legs and turn toward her, eager for a lesson in taming my temper. "That's my problem. I feel as if my sharp words will cut me to pieces if I don't let them cut someone else. And then I keep speaking before I even know what I'm saying and if I know I'm hurting someone, I'll keep going because I know I'm telling the truth— and I feel like that's worth it. How do you do it?"

"My good mother used to help me—"

"As you do us," I interrupt and lean forward to kiss her cheek.

She beams. "But I lost her when I was a little older than you are. For years, I had to struggle alone because I was too proud to confess this weakness to anyone else. I had a hard time. Then, your father came along and I was so happy, I forgot to be angry. But, then I had four little daughters and we were poor and... I'm not patient by nature."

"What helped you then?"

"Your father," she says in a sad voice. "He never loses patience, never doubts nor complains, but always hopes, and works and waits so cheerfully. He helped and comforted me to be the best example for you girls, for your sakes are more motivating than my own."

"Oh, Marmee. If I'm even half as good as you, I'll be happy," I say as I sink back into her arms as if I'm six years old again and small instead of tall and lanky. I'll never be too old or too big to crawl into my mother's arms.

"I hope you'll be a great deal better. You must watch over your temper, for it can spoil your life if you let it. Try with heart and soul to master this quick temper before it brings you worse sorrow than today."

I look up at her. "I'm going to try. But can you help me, remind me, and keep me from flying out? You said Father helped you."

"Yes, I asked him to help me so, and he never forgot it."

A sudden memory weaves into my mind—of Christmas a few years ago when everyone was home and we had an abundance of gifts. When we were all happy.

"I miss him."

A melancholic tinge glimmers in her eyes. "I do, too, my love."

Then the memory of the day he left us surfaces, front and center and as vivid as ever. That dark day still haunts me, but I force myself to remember, for it's the last day I saw my father's face outside a dream. "You told him to go—and didn't cry when he went nor do you complain. How do you do it? Such a brave sacrifice?"

She hums. "Because I want to contribute toward a future in this country where everyone can feel safe no matter who they are or identify as."

Before I can respond, Amy stirs, her tired voice squeaking, "Jo?"

I jolt up and rush to the bedside, tripping over my skirt in the process. "Ames? Are you okay? What do you need?"

Her eyes, half-closed, flutter as she shuffles in the blankets until her arms are free. She holds them out to me and I fly into her embrace. With a single, hearty kiss on her round cheek, everything starts anew.

"Jo, oh, Jo, come quick!" Marmee calls from the bottom of the attic steps.

In a flurry, I rush to her with a frightened heart until I see the smile on her face. "What is it?"

She takes my hand and guides me downstairs. In the parlor, where Beth's old and half-broken piano should be, sits a shiny new one.

"Where the dickens did that come from?" I ask.

"It's for Beth," Meg exclaims, "from Mr. Laurence!"

My heart swells. Oh, she's going to love it! I already know how she'll react—disbelief, red cheeks. She'll be so grateful that it won't look like she's grateful at all because it'll stun her into silence and no words will properly show how happy she is.

"She's coming!" Amy shouts, looking at the open window. "Beth! Beth! He sent you—"

My hand over Amy's mouth smothers the rest of the statement. "Let her be surprised!"

Beth hurries inside and we crowd around her. I'm so excited as if I've been given a library of my own. She is often forgotten by others but is the very heart of this family. As I suspected, she falls into silence. Her eyes widen and her jaw drops at the sign on the piano that reads *Miss Elizabeth March*.

I take her basket with her doll and set it aside. Beth walks closer, then turns to us. "For me?" she whispers, reaching toward me. I let her cling to my arm as reality settles in for her.

"Yes, all for you, my precious. Isn't it so kind? He's the sweetest, dearest old man in the world! Here—here's the key and the letter."

"We didn't open it," Marmee says. "But we're dying to know what he wrote for you."

"Oh, you read it, Marmee!" Beth exclaims, hiding her face in my neck. "It's too lovely and kind, I can't handle it!"

Mother opens the letter and I wrap my arms around my sister as the letter is read.

"Dear Madam,

I have had many pairs of slippers in my life, but I never had any that suited me so well as yours. Those are my favorite flowers and will always remind me of the gentle giver. I like to pay my debts, so I know you will allow this old gentleman to send you something which once belonged to the little child he lost. With hearty thanks and best wishes, I remain

Your grateful friend and humble servant,

James Laurence."

Amy can't stop gushing about how elegant and old-fashioned the note sounds while Marmee and Hannah urge Beth to give the piano a try. In all my days, I've never seen Beth as happy and content as today.

CHAPTER 11

RIVERS, CLOSETS, AND CHICKENS

When spring rolls around, my sisters and I love to stay outside.

One blossoming afternoon, while I'm in the coop to feed the chickens, I spot Laurie, Beth, and Amy around the redbud tree. Laurie latches onto a branch to shake the tree loose of any lingering magenta petals. Flowers begin raining on Beth and Amy, who lock hands and spin together. Their skirts fly about them and I smile at their girlish laughter.

Once I return to feeding the animals, Laurie appears behind me. "What d'you have there?"

"Teddy! Come in. I want you to meet my chicken, Aunt Cockle-top." I point to her and, though Laurie enters the coop, he says far from the roaming animals.

"Please keep that from me," he says, shaking some magenta flower petals from his curls as he skirts away.

"Don't be afraid," I exclaim, cleaning my hands on my linen apron before scooping up Aunt Cockle-top. She flaps her wings.

Teddy stumbles backward. "Jo!"

"She's just a chicken. Face your fears!" I haul Aunt Cockle-top into the air toward him.

He yelps and loses his footing without trying to catch her. My chicken falls on top of him and he screeches, "She bit me!" to send me into a deep laughing fit.

"Josephine!" Marmee's scolding voice startles me. My laughter is slow to dissipate as she brings a whimpering Laurie inside.

Later that week, Meg and I tend to the garden together. Gardening is a magnificent way for her to distract her mind from the blunder during her week at the Moffat's. When she told Marmee and me about it, she had us swear to never tell anyone. The secret aches inside me, but I cannot properly describe what Meg felt during that week, so I shall leave it to her to expand upon.

"Whoa there!" a voice calls. "Do I see Jo March in a garden? Tending to flowers?"

I look up to see Laurie perched on the wood fence with the grassy field leading to his mansion behind him. Amy and Beth are off elsewhere and Meg works diligently in her little plot without sparing our fellow curly-haired friend a glance.

"Yes, and I'm very excited about my sunflowers this year!" I exclaim as he walks over. "The seeds are going to feed Aunt Cockle-top and her chicks." At the mention of our chicken, he caresses his wounded hand from the other day. I plant my dirty hands on my hips. "Ha! Are you scared of a little chicken?"

"No!" he insists, but I see the fearful memory in his eyes and I laugh. He shakes it off. "Come on, let's go rowing."

I slump my shoulders. "No! My arms are still sore from last time."

He chuckles and reaches toward me with a tilt of his head because he knows I won't deny him. I puff and ignore his offered hand. "Fine. But it's *your* turn to row." I clean my hands off on my dark blue-and-red plaid skirt. "Meg, want to come?"

My older sister doesn't look up as she spreads around soil and takes the watering can. "No, thank you."

Laurie walks ahead and glances at me expectantly. I follow him toward the river. The cloudless sky is a welcoming shade of blue, vast and empty, waiting for opportunities. Spring is my favorite season, for everything is in bloom. Green leaves come out to say hello again, and rivers rush, filling the earth with enough water to grow beginnings.

Despite the blooming world, the chill hasn't vanished. I squeeze warmth into my cold nose with my fingers. Laurie darts down the hill toward the water where the abandoned canoe awaits us.

"Hey, wait for me!" I call and chase after him. I stumble to a stop when he turns around in such a sudden motion that I slam into his chest. "*Oof—!*"

"Watch where you're going," he teases. Before I can protest, his slender fingers glide over my face. I flinch and swat him away.

"Hey—what are you—"

"Stand still!"

We swat each other's hands. "Why are you touching my fa—"

Laurie cuts me off by taking my face in his hand. My cheeks smoosh under his fingertips. His eyes sparkle with amusement as he looks at my scrunched-up face.

"Stop," he says, fighting to withhold a laugh. "You have dirt on your face." He releases me and pinches my nose once more. I wipe the same spot.

"You could have just told me," I mutter, walking toward the canoe.

"Where's the fun in that?"

I fail to understand why wiping dirt from my face would be fun, but I don't say anything. The river flows in a peaceful trickle before me. I pluck out some of the fallen leaves and plop into my usual spot. When I look up, Laurie stands outside the boat, a daisy in hand. A hesitant look crosses his face. He twirls the green stem between his fingers as the puffy white sleeves of his shirt ruffle in the breeze.

"What are you doing?" I ask as I bounce my leg. "The waters are waiting."

He doesn't reply and walks closer instead. He holds the daisy toward me.

I lift a brow. "What's this for?"

"You."

I straighten my spine. My birthday passed and a gift-giving holiday isn't for a while. Besides, a flower as a gift is... neither what I'd want nor ask for.

"Why?" Now it's my turn to twirl the stem between my fingers.

"Because you love daisies."

This is true, but—

"Why would you pick it?"

At this, he chuckles and begins to push the canoe off the shore. He steps inside and uses the oar to push us out further. "Because I wanted to give a pretty thing to a pretty girl." He begins rowing in a steady rhythm.

A pretty thing to a pretty girl. The explanation still doesn't add up. What does that accomplish? Why pick a flower?

"You're weird, Teddy," I say with a shake of my head, tossing the flower into the river. I'm not sure what he wants me to do with it. He gives a short laugh in response. As the boat floats downstream, the sun blinds me and the breeze wafts loose curls over my eyes. This is what I get for not telling Marmee where I'm going. She would have told me to bring a hat.

"Jo," Laurie says in the quiet. At my humming response, he asks, "Why do you hate romance?"

"What are you talking about?"

He stops rowing and rests his elbows on his knees. "Or—sentiment as you call it. You don't ever seem to show interest in becoming part of society. Or making a match or finding some dashing suitor to sweep you off your feet."

"I don't like being swept off my feet. It makes me feel unstable."

Laurie laughs despite my serious tone and demeanor. "Seriously," he says. "I mean—don't you think about the future?"

He should know that I think of it every day. My dreams of becoming a successful writer of novels and short stories are the reasons I get out of bed. "All the time. I think about being a writer—"

"And that's it? Life as a writer—*alone*?"

"Why all these questions?" I blurt. The chirping birds calmed me a moment ago. Now they're a burden to my thoughts.

"I'm asking who you see in your future, that's it!" He straightens his spine and resumes rowing. "I don't know why you're getting so worked up about it."

"I'm not getting worked up about it."

"You are."

"Am not!"

"Jo—"

"No, Teddy," I interrupt, shooting to my feet. "Why all these sentimental questions? You *always* ask me these things! Why I don't go to parties or meet your friends or start showing interest in making a match! I'm *more* than that, Theodore Laurence—"

"*I know*—"

"Then why don't you ever ask me about anything else? You never ask about my writing or my stories—only stupid things!"

"Love isn't stupid!" he insists, glaring up at me.

"What you ask about isn't love! It—it's about control and—and expectations! Why am I expected to marry?"

He sputters.

"*Why?*" I demand, hands on my hips.

"Because it's what's done!"

"Because that's what society *said* should be done!"

Laurie releases a loud groan. "My God, Jo! It's okay to want something that everyone else does!"

"I never said I wanted it!"

"Then what *do* you want?"

"To be a writer!"

"You *are* a writer!"

"Not good enough," I say, crossing my arms over my chest. "I'll be good enough when my best friend asks about my books before he asks about my love life."

He scoffs. "You know I care about your writing."

I throw my arms in the air. "You never act like it."

"So you're upset I don't give enough attention to your work?"

"And *you're* upset I don't give enough attention to stupid things?"

The height of the argument begins to settle. After my manuscript was ruined, he didn't seem all that grieved for me. He let me roam his library, but I'm beginning to think he does things like that to make himself look good rather than wanting me to be happy.

I huff, cross my arms again, and plop back down. Laurie laces his fingers together.

"I'll start showing more interest in your writing—and you'll start showing more interest in love?"

"No! Yours is stupid."

He balks. "That's not fair!"

"You're a boy, Teddy. Love is a hobby to you and *supposed* to be a life for me."

"But do you *want* love?"

I've seen the way Mother and Father love—the way they argue, the way they have such control over the other's emotions. It doesn't appeal to me—giving another your heart and being at their mercy. They can stomp all over it one day without warning. It's better, more logical, to pour love into something you can control. Like writing.

"What I *want* is to be a respected enough woman where love is not a constant topic of conversation."

Laurie sits back and clenches his jaw. His nostrils flare. "I am going to hit you with this oar, Josephine March."

I lean closer and turn my cheek toward him. "Do it."

"WHY ARE WE IN A CLOSET?"

"Because they'll be here soon."

"But that—"

"I have to introduce the idea first," I explain. "They might not like a boy being part of the *Pickwick*, but if you're already here waiting..."

Darkness masks his face, but I can tell his brows lift with skepticism. "Got it..."

Our legs weave together and fresh air flows through the small crack in the door. Slivers of the sun leak inside. We haven't spoken much since our tiff on the river, but we gloss over those arguments every time. Dust floats in the stream of light splitting the space between our faces. My fingers dance in the sunbeam, a stark contrast to my shadowed wrist. Laurie does the same. Our fingers dance together. We fall into a routine; my pinky leans forward, his pinky leans back. The routine flows back and forth between our fingers until we lose rhythm. Giggles bubble between us, our orange-tinted skin grazing together.

I pull my hand away and lower my chin onto his bent knee. No one knows that I went into town to give an editor one of my short stories. The agony of waiting rips me apart and I want Laurie to be my solace—as he always is. But the day I went to the office, I remember spotting him at a billiard saloon.

"I saw you at the billiard saloon," I whisper, gazing up at him. "Why were you there?"

He leans his head against the wall. "I wasn't at a billiard saloon."

"Yes, you were. I saw you." I place my hands under my chin. "A fellow with a green hat always sits outside."

"Oh—that wasn't a saloon!" he exclaims, earning a hush from me. "It was a gymnasium. I've been taking lessons in fencing."

Relief breaks free in my chest. Boys who play billiards are no good and I have high expectations for my boy. "I'm glad—you can teach me." I squeeze his knees. "And then we can play Hamlet and you'll be Laertes."

A smile pulls at his lips. "We don't have to play Hamlet for me to teach you. But I don't believe that was your only reason for saying *I'm glad* in that way, was it?"

I release a sigh and sit back. "No, I was glad you weren't in the saloon because I don't want you to go to such places."

"It's no harm. I have billiards at home, but it's boring without good players. I play sometimes with Ned or some of the other fellows."

His attempt to reduce my anxiety about it only worsens the situation. "Oh—no! Teddy, you *mustn't* play billiards or remain with Ned and his set. You'll get to liking it better and better and you'll waste time and grow into those dreadful boys. I do want you to stay respectable."

He flinches. "Can't a fellow take a little innocent amusement now and then without losing his respectability?"

"It depends. Maybe. But I don't like Ned and his set and wish you'd keep out of it. Marmee doesn't like them and won't let them over. If you become like them, I won't see you any —*shh.* I think they're coming..." I peek toward the crack, but no one creaks up the garret steps. "No, false alarm."

When I settle back in my spot, silence falls over us until Teddy breaks it. "So, what have you been writing?"

I bite the inside of my cheek. I perk and lean closer. "Can you keep a secret?"

He smiles and leans closer to match me. "Always."

"I went to *The Spread Eagle* and left two stories with the editor. He's going to give me an answer next week."

"Are you serious!" he exclaims, gripping my shoulders. "Hurrah for Miss Mar—"

I clamp my hand over his mouth with a laugh. "Hush, they might hear! And it won't come to anything, but I couldn't rest until I'd tried and I haven't said anything because I don't want to disappoint people."

He takes my hand in his and stares into my eyes across the sunbeam between us. "It won't fail, Jo. Your stories are works of Shakespeare compared to the rubbish they publish every day." He kisses the back of my hand. "It's going to be so great to see your work in print and I'll feel proud of my authoress."

Warmth spreads through my chest. The thought of someone outside of my family believing in me is affirming and comforting —especially from Teddy. Typically, I let confidence reign. I would lift my chin and brace for whatever happens, but hints of hopeful tears press against my eyes. "Really?"

He nods. "Really."

In a rush of emotion, I lurch forward and kiss him on the cheek as I've done to my family plenty of times. "Thank you, my boy." Before either of us can speak, my sisters trample up the stairs for our family newspaper meeting. "Oh—they're here! Remember, when I stomp three times, that's your cue."

"Understood."

I roll out of the closet and close the door, spreading my arms wide. "Welcome, welcome, gentlemen! Who's ready to talk about *The Pickwick Portfolio?*"

CHAPTER 12

IMMORTAL FLOWERS

Beth adores playing postmistress for the house and handing out our mail. But one morning, she walks in with a bouquet.

"Who sent *those?*" Meg asks from her spot sewing on the couch.

I'm sitting at the kitchen table jotting down a few story ideas. Indeed, cradled in Beth's arms is a large bouquet of begonias. The pink flowers glisten as she passes a window through which the sun streams.

"Laurie did," Beth says, stopping at Meg's side. "Here's your letter and a glove."

She lifts a brow. "Just one glove?"

I look at the flowers. "Teddy probably sent those for me. He's been trying to—"

"No, they're for Marmee," Beth interjects. "And yes, Meg. Just one."

"For *Marmee?*"

While, of course, there is nothing but motherly affection behind the flowers Laurie sent her, I hate the jealous twinge that levels in my gut. It became almost a steady routine of my best friend trying to reflect romantic sentiments among our days.

"Oh, I hate to have odd gloves!" Meg exclaims as she opens the letter. "Never mind, I'm sure it's around here somewhere. My letter is only a translation of the German song I wanted. I think Mr. Brooke did it, for this isn't Laurie's writing."

Marmee is situating the begonias in a vase when she says my name and points toward the window. Laurie's brown face appears, jovial and smiling as he beckons me outside. I clean the ink from my hands before stepping into the warm afternoon. I'm wearing a thin blouse with a yellow vest, paired with a tan skirt. My hair twists into a long braid down my back as usual.

Laurie and I walk through the garden, up and down the rows. Bugs flitter around my sunflowers. Cicadas screech in the plants and trees. "You sent Marmee flowers," I say and turn around to look at him.

He slides his hands into his pockets. "I did."

"Why?"

"Because she likes them."

I don't reply and continue walking through the plants. My hands graze over the leaves and brush against the petals.

"You want flowers, too, don't you?"

I whirl on him. "What—"

"I can send you some—"

"No," I insist, "why would I want that?" I pull myself up straight and realize how much I don't want romantic sentiments. The thought makes me squirm. "Flowers are pretty, but they should stay in gardens. They'll just wither and die and then I'll be sad. There's no point for it."

I pass him and head for the house, but he stops me and says, "Some English girls and boys are coming to see me tomorrow and I want you girls to come. If it's okay, I'm going to pitch my tent in Longmeadow for lunch and croquet—have a fire, make messes, and all sorts of larks." He speaks quicker. "They're nice and they like such things. Brooke will go and keep us boys from being too rowdy. I want you all to come, even Beth. She can sit aside and no one shall worry her if that's what she wants. Don't bother about rations, I'll see to that and everything else. I only want you all to join."

Amy and Meg will be ecstatic. I don't wish to meet more of his friends, but it's a sacrifice I must make for my boy and my sisters. I flex my hands in an attempt to rid my nerves. "You won't be trying to find me a match, will you?"

The corner of his lips quirks. "Never."

I can't hide my smile. "Good."

LAURIE CALLED THE EVENT *CAMP LAURENCE*.

Beth sat off to the side most of the time and Meg stayed in conversation with Mr. Brooke. Amy and I were more involved with everyone, including my almost-thrashing of Fred Vaughn for cheating at croquet.

My sisters and I finished dinner and relax in the parlor, chatting about the day. Beth tells us that she had a conversation with one of the Vaughn boys—the nicer one.

Meg disappears upstairs to prepare for bed, much tired from the day's affairs while Amy and Beth remain. I head toward the attic to start writing when I spot an envelope with my name on the doormat.

I turn over the unblemished paper that holds no hints about how long it's been here. Inside is a watercolor painting on thick paper. The blue and pink and red flowers have immaculate detail, blossoming with eternal beauty. I don't recognize the signature of the artist. But on the back is Laurie's handwriting.

FOR JO—
THESE FLOWERS WILL NEVER DIE.
EVER YOURS,
TEDDY

My chest tightens and tears prick my eyes. *Oh, Teddy,* is all I can think. *Why? Why me?* Sniffling, I pack up the envelope and head to my bedroom to change into my night shift. I don't feel like writing anymore. Meg sits on the ground braiding her hair.

"Did you have fun today?" I ask to distract my mind from the irritatingly kind gift Laurie sent me. I begin to unbraid my own hair.

She hums through a soft smile, fingers lacing through her hair. "I did. Mr. Brooke is sweet, is he not?"

"He's very smart."

"He was telling me about Wampanoag traditions. It's so interesting..." Her voice has a dreamy hint to it. Why is everyone getting such romantic notions? *There must be something in the air,* I convince myself as Meg adds, "I've never met anyone like him before."

I suppress a groan as I fall on my back across the bed, my hair dangling over the edge. My head rests beside my sister's.

"Gigi," I begin, biting my lip while she toys with her brown strands. My use of her rare nickname must snap her back to reality, for I feel her eyes on my cheek. I stare at the ceiling, not daring to meet her gaze for my next confession. "I fear Teddy has feelings for me."

"Why do you fear? Don't you like him back?"

"Of course not."

"How come? He adores you."

"And *I* adore *him!*" I reply, then hesitate. "I don't know. We would make a horrid match. You see how we argue."

She tugs at my curls. "I think he could make you happy."

"He already does!" It baffles me that Meg hints at something more than friendship between me and the boy across the way. He makes me happy *now* and I don't understand why that's not enough for everyone. "I don't want things to change."

"And what are *things?*" she asks. "Him doting on you, sending you gifts?"

My stomach twists. I hate the idea of him leaving me alone —of him never flirting or calling me pretty or making me feel special. A groan escapes my lips and I cover my face. "It's horrible, isn't it? I'm horrible."

Meg places an elbow on the bed and a hand on my shoulder. "You're not horrible, Jo. We're girls. We like being doted on." I watch her tilt her head with a quizzical look. "But you don't want to dote back? Send him something? Make him smile?"

I hesitate, searching my mind and heart for that desire, but I come up with nothing. "Not... not really. Well, not in a sentimental, romantic way."

She glances away in thought. "Okay, what do you *want* to happen?" She shakes her head. "Ignore what's right and wrong. Just what your heart wants."

"I don't want him, but I also don't want him to want anyone else..." I sigh. "I want to be loved, but *I* don't want to love. I... can't."

"Everyone can love," Meg says in a soft voice.

I shake my head. "Not in that way. I've tried, Gigi. I've tried to... love Teddy in the way everyone wants me to, but... I don't think I can." Tears prick my eyes. "And if I can't love a boy who gives me everything, then how can I love at all?"

My older sister grazes her hand over my forehead and down my hair in a mother-like fashion. "Love him in *your* way. If he can't accept that... well, he'll have to. A life of unrequited feelings from Jo March is better than life without her friendship."

I sniffle, fighting to keep in the tears. My voice cracks. "Am I truly worth that?"

She presses her forehead against mine. "Every bit of it."

THE BUSY BEE SOCIETY SITS UNDER A SHADED TREE ON A warm, late-summer day. In my pocket sits my published short story folded up into a dozen squares. Amy sketches a group of ferns, Meg sews, and Beth designs a flower crown as I read aloud. I often stumble over the words as I keep pondering how to tell them about my published work.

Hi, I'm published!

Want to read a story? I wrote it!

Here, I shall read a different story and—

No, too much thinking. I should come right out with it. "I have something to—"

"There's Laurie!" Amy interjects.

Indeed, Teddy saunters up to us with his hands stuffed into his pockets. He flashes a soft smile. "May I join?"

Meg nods to the open spot on the blanket. "Of course, but you must be of use to the Busy Bee Society."

When he lowers across from me and crosses his legs, an idea jumps into my mind. "Oh, I know! He can read another story. This one bored me, anyway and I can knit while he reads."

I hand him the folded newspaper clipping. Laurie clears his throat and begins reading in a confident tone, telling the tale of Viola and Angelo as star-crossed lovers. In a fictional land ravaged by war and hate, they ventured across the many battle-fields to proclaim their love and discover its true meaning. Romance does nothing for me in real life, but I confess I find a level of contentment in both reading and writing it.

It has a profound impact on my sisters. Amy stops her

sketching and gazes toward the river, lost in the story as she clings to every word that falls from Laurie's lips. Beth watches him with the utmost attention, her chin plopped onto her folded knees as her brow quirks and her lip quivers every time an intense scene occurs. Meg, despite her continuing to work, is the most affected of them all. She sews with vigor while trying to hide her watering eyes.

"Wait," Laurie says as he reaches the end. "They all died?"

"What a splendid picture," Amy muses. "Even though it was sad."

"But it was amazing," Beth chirps.

Meg wipes her eyes. "It was; I loved it. Who wrote it?"

Laurie holds up the paper again and squints. "Someone named—*J. March!*" His eyes snap to me. "Jo! This is yours!"

"What?" Amy asks.

"Really?" Beth asks.

"But it's published!" Meg exclaims.

Silence topples over the group. I sit tall, my chin held high. A moment later, my sisters lurch forward and throw their arms around me with their exclaims of pride.

Meg: "Oh, Jo!"

Beth: "I'm so happy!"

Amy: "Finally!"

Laurie reaches across the picnic blanket and nudges my leg with his foot. "A published author! You're so official!"

"Thank you," I say without realizing how sheepish I truly am over the whole ordeal. I didn't think I would adopt modesty through this publication since my first few stories were rejected months ago. "I'm glad you like it."

"We love it," Beth promises, squeezing my knee before settling back on her end of the blanket. "Oh, do write some more. I'm sure they'll publish it."

"I will, dear. Promise." My face warms. "It's... a dream come true."

Amy snatches my wrist, ambition glistening in her pale eyes. "*We* will be the famous ones, Jo. Watch us make the family rich beyond reason!"

Despite her clear wish for money and status, it's lovely to see such talent in my youngest sister. Ambition is the most important quality to have. I bring Amy into my arms. She reclines between my legs, her back against my chest.

"That is not my goal, but certainly would be nice," I tell her. I turn to Meg. "What's *your* goal?"

Her gaze wanders to the river and the wishes fall off her lips as if prepared for this question. "I should like... a lovely house, full of all sorts of luxurious things—nice food, pretty clothes, handsome furniture, pleasant people, and heaps of money. I'll be mistress of it and manage it as I want, with plenty of servants so I won't work too much. How I should enjoy it! I wouldn't be idle, but I would do enough to make everyone love me dearly."

I snort. "And what about all the little snot-nosed children running about?"

An offended look passes over her face. She squares her shoulders and returns to sewing while pulling on a haughty air. "*Pfft.* You'd have nothing but inkstands and novels and animals in yours."

"How marvelous that sounds!" I exclaim, though she means this as an insult. "I'll have stables and pig pens and my own gigantic library and magical inkstands and my works should be as famous as Amy's art. I want to do something splendid before I die. Something heroic so I won't be forgotten."

The thought of my potential home fills me with comfort. For a fleeting moment, I think of Teddy. What if he was there? It could be fun, filled with joy and jokes. But as we grew, and had children, he would expect me to do all of the caretaking. He would bring his friends over, the ones I don't like, and it would be a constant quarrel. He would wonder why I didn't stop writing to cook for them and I would wonder why I ever thought we would have a good marriage.

Any thought of having a courtship with Theodore Laurence flees my mind once and for all.

Amy clears her throat. "*I* want to be an artist and go to Rome and do fine pictures so I can be the best artist in the whole world!"

It's a future I can easily see for her. Laurie nudges Beth. "And what about you, Beth?"

She startles as if surprised we want to hear her dreams. "Oh, I want to stay home safe with Mother and Father and help take care of the family."

"Really?" I ask. "Nothing more?"

Beth shrugs. "I've got my piano. I'm content."

Perhaps it's my overly ambitious nature, considering I haven't ever met someone with as many dreams and goals as me —except Amy. "Teddy? Your dreams?"

Laurie shrugs too. "I want to travel. See as much of the world as I can. Then, I'll settle in Germany and have as much music as I want. I'll be a famous musician. I'll never be bothered about money or business. I'll enjoy myself and those I love."

In an instant, Teddy shows his lovable parts. Despite his haughty nature, he invites the world into his life and wants to swallow as much of it as possible. "That's a good dream," I say. "I would advise you to sail away in one of your ships and never come home again until you've tried your own way!"

Laurie smiles in agreement.

"That's not right, Jo. You mustn't talk in that way!" Meg exclaims, then dives into a motherly rant about the right thing for him to do, which makes the rest of us nod off.

Chapter 13

Lovesickness

The days grow chilly and Concord begins to bid summer farewell for the year. I lose myself in writing up in the garret. Stories occupy my mind for days on end. Scrabble is my loyal companion and endures a couple of my scolding rants when he scurries across the overhead beams too loudly.

Writing, in my not-so-humble opinion, is the most beautiful art form. It is the painting of the words and lips. A writer can concoct a sentence that has no logical meaning, but the flow of words sounds like music. Rewrites, ripping pages, crossing out words; it's one of the most prolific times in the dawn of my career. Short stories and poetry float down a stream from my brain to my fingertips, and sometimes to my lips when I must speak the words aloud to parse them onto paper.

The novels I work on are the hardest. They require attention I can give them but a few days of the week. Novel plots take specific tweaking because the stories are much too vast to mess up. For the sake of my hands, it is preferable to work through the plot well enough before I begin writing it to reduce the number of rewrites.

A couple of times, Marmee trudges up the stairs and forces my pinafore off me to clean it. This leads to some of my other clothes getting stained with ink. Character names jumble in my mind day in and day out. Stories cross paths and I find myself writing Jane's story on Charlotte's pages and have to start over completely.

Marmee sends up Laurie to try and convince me to join the world, but he ends up joining my world every time. He helps me work through my story and listens to my ideas and complaints and sits without a protest when I snap at him for talking as I jot down a note before I forget it.

Laurie picks up one of my short stories bound with a red ribbon. "*Pirate Jane*," he reads. "What's this one about?"

I glance up from my desk as I scribble through Charlotte's story. "Huh—oh, that's about a girl pirate who leads a crew and ambushes British ships that stole artifacts from other countries and returns them to their rightful homes."

He hums. "They won't publish this."

"What?" I ask, half distracted. "Why wouldn't they?"

"Americans love the British. This is too radical for most."

I reach over and snatch the story to place it back where he got it from. "It's a good thing I write for myself, then. I don't write to please others."

"It would be okay if you did, though."

"It doesn't matter because I *don't*." I clean off the tip of my pen and re-dip it into the ink.

"Why not?"

I continue scribbling through Charlotte's story—the scene where she tells the knight she doesn't need him to save her. I mutter a distracted response, "Because I live by my own rules."

"Can I read it?"

"Go ahead. Don't wrinkle the pages."

I slip back into Charlotte's story. Now, she has a sword and battles the dragon herself. Once I finish her story, where the dragon dies and she lives happily ever after with the knight, I let the ink dry while I search for more ribbon.

"That was phenomenal, Jo!"

I jump, almost forgetting that Laurie is even here. With my long braid messy and my pinafore crooked, I rise and turn to him. "You like it?"

Laurie reclines on the chaise, the pages of my story in hand, with one arm thrown behind his head. He stares down his body at me with a grin. "You have ink on your nose. But yes! I love this. Publishers would be stupid not to accept it. It's riveting and fresh."

A grin stretches across my face as a rush of confidence floods through me. I hop onto the end of the sofa. Laurie bends his legs and I lean forward, pressing against his knees to stare down at him. "You promise?"

He chuckles. "I promise." He removes his arm from behind his head to realign the pages. "You want to hear a secret?"

"Always."

"He told me not to tell anyone but everyone knows you're not included in my promise of telling no one."

"Yes, of course." I shake his knees. "What is it?"

"I know where Meg's glove is."

I blink, trying to pull up the memory of Meg even losing a glove. "What do you mean?"

"That I know where Meg's glove is," he repeats.

"*How?* Why?"

"Because I know the fellow who has it."

"A fellow? Did someone steal it? Oh, I should hurt them!" I shake his knees again, harder than before. "Tell me!"

He smirks. "John Brooke."

A gasp escapes me as I lean closer. "What? How do you know?"

"Saw it."

"Where?"

"Pocket. Then he showed me."

"All this time?"

"Yes, isn't that romantic?"

I groan and fall back onto my rear. "How is stealing a girl's glove romantic? It's horrid!"

"Don't you like it?" Laurie asks as he sits up.

"Of course not! It's ridiculous and won't be allowed." I clamp my hands over my ears. If only I could pull the words from my memory and forget it ever happened. "Oh, what will Meg say?"

He snatches my wrist. "You are *not* to tell anyone."

"I never promised such a thing!"

"C'mon, Jo!"

I yank my wrist back and fold my arms across my chest. My hand still aches from all this writing and I fear that Teddy stole all of my writing inspiration. I'm much too sad to write now. My days and weeks have been spent cooped up in the garret! I should be at Meg's side as often as I can. John Brooke may steal her away and I'll never see her again. "Okay, fine, my boy, but I'm disgusted and I wish you hadn't told me."

"I thought you'd be pleased."

"What on earth would give you that idea! I don't want anyone coming to take Meg away!" I stand to search for the ribbon I'd originally risen for. My heart feels leaden.

Teddy wraps his arms around me from behind, laughing as I try to fend him off. "You'll feel better about it when somebody comes to take you away."

"*Pfft,*" I huff, shoving him off and spinning to face him. "I'd like to see anyone try it."

He removes a handkerchief from his pocket and dabs it on

his tongue; taking my chin in his hand, he begins to wipe the ink off my face. "So should I, my little writer! So should I."

I TRY TO CONTAIN MYSELF IN THE COMING DAYS, BUT MY temper reigns.

Every time Mr. Brooke comes around, I lift my nose and turn away. Rudeness becomes me and my family takes notice. Their stares linger; they don't say anything. Sometimes, I find myself staring at Meg. She's growing up. We're *all* growing up and I hate the idea that she will have kids of her own, a house of her own, a family of her own. I know we spoke of our futures not too long ago, but it's all happening so much quicker than I anticipated. I'll be left behind and she'll forget about me.

My solace is with Laurie. Every day, I escape the tension and fight to ignore the ever-changing household by spending time with him. When I spot him in the garden one day, eagerness overtakes me and I don't even run to the door; I climb out the window. Meg gasps; I ignore her and continue toward my boy.

"If I tag you, you have to write me a poem!" he calls, running toward me.

I take off in the other direction, wading through the decaying garden. The overcast gives me no brightness, no sun. The quick beating of my heart and the pumping of my legs warm me in an instant. He almost catches me a couple of times. When he finally does, it's behind the big tree Amy usually sits under during warm weather. Now it's just us hidden from sight. Laurie wraps an arm around my waist and presses me into the tree trunk.

"A poem, please."

My laughter dissipates and I push him off me. I haven't

written since he told me about Meg and Mr. Brooke. "I don't want to."

He notices my hesitation. "What's wrong? Are you still out of sorts since I told you about Meg's glove?"

My gaze jumps to his at his irritated tone. "Yes, as a matter of fact, I am! I don't think secrets agree with me. I feel rumpled up in my mind. I don't want things to change."

"Change is good," he says, sliding his hands into his pockets.

I crinkle my nose. "Liar."

"You're almost sixteen. It's time to think about these things."

"Why are you in such a rush to grow up?" I ask, folding my arms.

"I'm not. I just know that it's coming."

"Doesn't mean you have to embrace it."

"Doesn't mean *you* have to reject it, either." Laurie huffs, swiping a hand over his mouth as if working through the correct words. "Honestly, Jo, what are you so afraid of?"

"I'm not afraid of anything."

"Who's the liar now?"

I drop my arms. "I'm not lying!"

"Are you afraid of love, is that it?"

"I'm not afraid of love—in fact, I'm tired of it!"

It's all I hear about! Especially from Laurie and Aunt March. Everyone is so concerned about making matches and having babies and I don't understand how and why these things are so important. They're especially important for women as if we're cows! Made for children and making food.

"For once, just let yourself have feelings."

I blink. "Teddy, why do I feel like you have such a wrong perception of me?"

I have many feelings. I have plenty of compassion, hope, and dreams. I care for my family more than anything. Teddy acts like romance is the most important feeling in the world and the truth is that it's not. He makes me feel broken—as if I was born the wrong way.

"Oh, please," he says. "I know you better than anyone."

"I don't think you do."

He stares at me for a moment. "Josephine March, you're afraid of change."

"No, I'm not," I lie.

"You're afraid that the world outside your family will hurt you."

Tears prick my eyes. It's like he sliced my chest open. It's too bare—too vulnerable and I don't like it. "Stop."

"You're afraid of giving your heart to someone because you think they'll—"

"Teddy!"

"You're afraid to trust—"

Anger bubbles in my gut. My hands stiffen from the cold; I point at him, anyway. "Teddy, I'm warning you."

"But you can trust *me*, Jo. You know—"

I shove his chest with a loud groan, not caring whether my voice can be heard from the house. "I am *not* some scared little girl in the dark who needs you—or anyone—to guide me into the light! I'm content where I am and I don't crave anything—"

"You're lying to yourself!" Laurie insists, stepping closer.

I lift my chin so we're nose to nose. "Stop acting like you know more than me! You're trying *so* hard to make me into—"

My heart lurches when his warm mouth covers mine. His cold nose brushes my cheek. Our lips slide together and every piece of my body is alight. Any chill flees my body, replaced with flames.

Teddy is kissing me.

My palm presses against his cheek and pushes him away. Blood sprints through my veins. My heart beats faster than it ever has. My fingers tremble and my throat tightens as if a sob is about to release. I don't understand what he's done to me—why my body invites him before consulting my logic. For the first time, I see the attraction of this—being joined with another. I don't know what to do with it; it's more than I can handle.

My fingers touch my lips and my head spins. I stare at him as he awkwardly looks at anything but me. I'm not in love with Theodore Laurence, but at this moment, I adore kissing him. I grab his face between my hands and pull him back to me. His body presses me into the tree trunk as his lips hungrily take mine. My arms wrap around his neck. Our mouths move in sync and my hand wanders up to his hair, clenching the curls. Words of protest shudder through my mind, but I banish them and listen to my gut—the piece of me that wants this even if I know it won't last long.

"JO! JO, COME QUICK!"

Meg's shrieking voice shocks me back to life. I shove Teddy away. Regret instantly replaces the desire. I shouldn't have kissed him. I don't want this—*us*.

"This never happened," I say, turning and sprinting toward Meg's fearful call.

CHAPTER 14

I'm Sick Of Love

Mrs. March:

Your husband is very ill. Come at once.

S. Hale
Blank Hospital, Washington

I can do nothing but stare at the note as everyone flies about around me. I don't remember Laurie following me inside, but I hear his voice. Marmee advises me to bring her pen and paper and only then do I snap out of it. She hates asking Aunt March for money. As Amy and Beth cry together and Meg stands dutifully at Marmee's side, awaiting instructions, I head to the front door.

Tears threaten my eyes. I wrap my cloak around my shoulders and gather my hair into a bonnet. Laurie stands in the foyer doorway.

"Where are you going?"

"I won't be long."

"Jo—"

"No, Teddy," I snap, a tear finally escaping as he walks toward me. "Not—not now. I-I can't—"

He brings me into a hug and I fall into sobs. My worst nightmare is around the corner. Papa might not come home ever again.

"It will be all right," he whispers.

"I—" I struggle to breathe. "I need your friendship right now, please. Forget it ever happened. Please."

"Of course. It's buried away. I'm always your dear friend."

I stand back and wipe away snot with my wrist. I don't give him another glance as I step outside, closer to chopping off my hair so we don't have to ask Aunt March for a single penny.

THE CHOPPING OF MY HAIR IS MET WITH CONFUSION AND shock. From Amy, a little contempt. It morphs into admiration, for I've sacrificed what makes a woman most beautiful on the outside. At least that's how Amy puts it. Before Marmee leaves, I find Meg and John Brooke in the kitchen alone. He offers to escort my mother to Washington, and it would fill me with gratitude if I didn't already know his true intentions. I don't let him leave without a withering glare.

Marmee takes off after giving each of us instructions, and we all try to keep them in mind as the days pass. Laurie treats the kiss as if it didn't happen and brings me books to distract my wandering mind from my father's potential demise.

Concord's November chill is more biting than ever before. The sharp winds can slice through unprotected bodies and I catch a cold from forgetting to cover my shorn head. This worries Laurie, but one pointed look from me and he reins in his emotions. He brings hot soup up to the garret—at least a quarter of it is always spilled. He once asks me whether I plan to keep my short hair, as he admits it's rather unbecoming. The question is met with my fist in his arm and a cough erupting from my chest. Amid my cold, I write plenty of stories and slide them to my sisters to lift their spirits.

Meg's seamless transition into the mother figure of the house unsettles me. She sits in Marmee's chair during meals and reminds us of our chores. It shows how ready and eager she is for a house and family of her own.

When Beth isn't sitting at the piano, she's at the Hummel's. It pleases me to see her out and about rather than cooped up inside. When Amy isn't drawing, she completes her studies, for she grows tired of mispronouncing and misspelling so many words. She admits she rather likes my shortened hair and, for a fleeting moment, considers chopping off her own until she remembers how slow her hair grows. Luckily, mine grows fast and will return to its original length within a year. My short curls give me no bother, but I do miss the warmth it provided me when I go outside to make snowmen with Amy. And I rather enjoyed having Meg fuss over how messy I let it get and when she combed and braided it for me. Perhaps I should break that routine because John Brooke is going to steal her from me soon.

Despite my unease at my sister's quick overtaking of Marmee's role, I admire her more as the days pass; she overflows with confidence and knowledge. Meg is everything I'm supposed to be and nothing I currently am. I admire her for being perfect, so I don't have to be. John Brooke is nowhere near good enough for her. One day, when Laurie is helping her clear the dinner table, I imagine them married. Once the image enters my mind, I embrace it. Meg is exactly who Laurie wants me to be. She's a right match for him! He can be polite and have manners when he wants, so I shouldn't worry about his hot temper.

The day I plan to introduce the idea to her, I pass Marmee's bedroom and hear a squeak and a sob. Beth sits crying in Mother's closet and my heart drops. Her duty is to collect the mail; what if she'd read a letter about Papa?

"Beth, what's wrong?" I ask, lowering before her and resting a hand on her knee. "Are Mother and Father all right?"

She nods and wipes her nose. "They're fine. You've—you've had scarlet fever, right?"

"Years ago, when Meg did. Why?" My response shakes Beth, for she leans forward and drops her head into my shoulder. Her sobs break my heart. "Beth, you're scaring me."

"Oh, Jo. The baby's dead!"

For a moment, fear seizes me, but then I realize I don't know a baby. "What baby?"

"Mrs. Hummel's. It died in my lap!"

"Oh, goodness. My poor dear, how dreadful!" I wrap my arms around her and graze a hand up and down her back.

"I saw right away the baby was sicker. The boy said Mrs. Hummel had gone to fetch the doctor, so I took the baby and let the boy rest. It seemed asleep, but it suddenly gave a cry, trembled, and then fell very still! And I knew it was dead, Jo. It was so young! It—it hadn't even said its first word."

As I console her, she tells me about the doctor's visit and her chances of having scarlet fever. She checked Marmee's book and learned she has the symptoms. It should have been me. Beth has asked me to go with her for days and I brushed her off to prioritize my writing.

My sister's red face and warm forehead send my nerves spiraling. I pace for minutes trying to calm myself. Washington is so very far away. If only Marmee were here... but the next adult is Hannah. When I fetch her, she makes the big decision and instructs Amy to stay at Aunt March's since she hasn't had the fever before.

As Hannah and I bring Beth to Marmee's comfortable bed,

Amy's protests echo from downstairs. Heavy footsteps thud upstairs and Laurie appears in the doorway of the bedroom. Hannah settles Beth under the quilt. I guide Laurie into the hallway and to the top of the steps.

"Is Beth okay?" he asks.

"I don't want to go!" Amy shouts from the parlor. "I want to stay here and help Beth!"

I sigh and run my palm over my forehead. "She's not feeling well. Mrs. Hummel's baby died in her arms and the doctor says she might have scarlet fever."

"That's why Amy's crying?"

"Yes. Can you visit her?" I ask. "I truly hate asking so much of you, Teddy. Ignoring what happened, helping us get on without Marmee, Father's illness, and now—"

"Your family has done so much for me," Laurie interrupts, taking both of my shoulders. "I should be glad to visit Amy if it will make your life easier and help Beth get better."

I throw my arms around his torso and lean my face into his neck. "Oh, thank you, my boy. I am forever grateful for you."

AFTER LAURIE TAKES AMY TO AUNT MARCH'S AND DR. Bangs examines Beth, we confirm that Beth has scarlet fever. It troubles her; she says she feels a burden because Mr. Laurence cannot visit her as usual and Meg stays home to refrain from infecting the Kings.

"Don't you worry about anything but getting better," I say while feeding her a spoonful of soup. Devoting myself to her day and night is the easiest task I am given. My sister is patient and bears her pain without complaint, even when her voice begins to worsen, and playing the piano ceases to lift her spirits.

Hannah writes letters to Marmee about the illness but

refuses to explain its severity. She says Marmee has enough worries, but Beth may benefit from seeing her. Rather than protest, I spend more time at my sister's side, as she doesn't like it when I let my temper fly.

My fears deepen when Beth's clarity begins to slip. She calls Meg *Marmee*, me *Meg*, and Hannah *Amy*. She often says the name Lucy, but none of us knows a Lucy. Meg, Hannah, and I try not to let our concerns show during our shifts of watching over her, for Beth hates to be worried about. It doesn't help to learn that Father had a relapse and is even sicker.

Days darken and hearts weigh heavy. During Meg's shifts, I hide in the garret. I have not even seen Scrabble in almost a week and all of my previous effort for writing is poured into my family. The attic is good for nothing other than sobbing. My heart cannot handle this cold loneliness and I am a ghost within my body. My soul is dampened, silenced, and all that grounds me is reading and holding Beth's hand.

One gray morning, when I'm dabbing Beth's sweaty face with a cloth, she speaks clearly and with intent for the first time in days.

"I have dreams," she says.

I take her hands with a hopeful heart. "What kind of dreams?"

"Beautiful dreams."

"Did you meet someone named Lucy?"

Beth's gaze loses focus. My heart stutters as I think she slips further away from the living. "Yeah," she whispers in a lulling tone. "Lucy."

"What does she look like?" I ask, but she blinks and continues staring into nothingness, a hint of a smile over her full lips. "Beth. Tell me what she looks like."

"Her hair... it's like the sun. Eyes like the ocean." She

releases a short breath like she's looking at something, or someone, otherworldly. "She loves me, Marmee."

I smile, a tear slipping onto my lip. I clear the fear and sorrow from my throat. "I'm sure she does. Where did you meet her?"

"The—the cottage. Our cottage." Beth inhales deeply, the raspy sound settling anguish in my heart.

I scrunch my face together in an effort to throw a wall up and stop the tears. "Okay, shh," I coo, brushing hair from her sweaty forehead. "Don't tire yourself out. No more talking."

But she trudges on. "We live"—she licks her dry, pale lips —"in a cottage. There are... mountains. Flowers, fresh air." She beams. "We have so many cats. She... Lucy likes to—bake pies while I..." She inhales again, raspier than before.

"No more talking, Beth." I dip the cloth in the bucket of water.

"While I play piano."

Tears slip down my cheeks as I press the damp cloth on her face. "*Shhh, shhh*. Rest now."

Later, Hannah and I switch roles. Standing in the kitchen with a hand on my hip, I stir the soup with a wooden spoon. Silent tears threaten to fall into the pot. Moments before, Dr. Bangs suggested we send for Marmee. I'm worn and heavy, donning the same skirt, blouse, and vest for the past three days. Curls escape from the French braid Meg had done for me. But I feel none of the exhaustion—only desperate fear.

Laurie enters through the back door and I swipe away the tears before he can see.

"I sent for Marmee," I say without sparing him a glance.

"Oh, good!" he exclaims. "You went ahead despite Hannah?"

I sniffle. "No. The doctor told us to."

His smile falters. "Oh, Jo, it's not that bad, is it?" His gentle hand comes to rest on my back and I stiffen.

"Yes, it is. Papa's doing better, but sickness will take him just as quickly if his—if his daughter—" I clamp a hand over my mouth to stifle a cry. He lurches forward and presses his chest into my shoulder, enveloping me in his arms. Tears stream fast from my eyes as I fall into my best friend. *My sister may die.* Those words break off pieces of my heart bit by bit, word by word. I'm a glass ball rolling to the edge of a table and I fear the drop. The past begins to solidify more with each moment. Beth is supposed to have time to grow out of her shell. Papa is supposed to have time to tell me about the war and live a tranquil life with his family. There should be more *time*.

Laurie whispers soothing words to me and I let him. So often, I adore pushing him away and I adore him continuing the effort. It's my favorite twisted game even though I know it won't last. But this is no game—Beth is dying and Marmee isn't here and Amy can't come home lest she falls ill and steps closer to death, too. I sob without relent, latching onto Laurie's coat sleeve and hiding my face in his shoulder because I know my expression is unsightly. I let anguish scratch from my throat in wails. Through my blurry eyes, I notice frost building on the window and snow falling to earth in a steady rhythm.

Annoyance builds in my gut. How can the world continue? The sun continues to set in purples and pinks and rises in blues and yellows while Beth is suffering. The world should stop and wait for her. Nothing can move on without her. She means more than that.

After minutes, when my head pounds and lungs fight to fill with air, I continue resting upon his chest to gather myself. Laurie's fingers brush against my hairline and tug strands from my eyes. He gives me a handkerchief and says, "Go be with her. I'll bring the soup."

I mend the fire in Marmee's room where Beth sleeps, relieving Hannah of her shift. Meg and I sit bedside, both of us lurching whenever she moves in the slightest. The goings-on of the world outside this room remains a mystery to me. Laurie and Hannah are the only others who enter the bedroom, often with gifts brought by the town. Hannah says that Mrs. Hummel arrived with begs of pardon, since she feels responsible. I want to agree; her family spread it to mine. She believed scarlet fever to be a mere cold and now her child is dead and my sister is close to it. Meg cuts into my rant and angry thoughts by placing her hand over mine.

"Think of how Marmee would react," she says. "She wouldn't blame Mrs. Hummel and you know it."

I lower my head in response. Many others stop by with condolences and prayers. The milkman, baker, grocer, and butcher—none of us knew that Beth has made so many friends. She's a loving sense of peace, the very heart of Concord, and it appears that they're not moving on without her.

CHAPTER 15

ONE SAVED, ONE GONE

Wintry days greet us.

Beth's illness rages, and Meg and I remain at her side, though Meg is often scribbling away on paper. At first, I believed she was writing in a journal; she has spurts of documenting her feelings. However, Hannah has been entering the room to take and deliver papers and envelopes.

As she scribbles at Marmee's desk, I finally ask, "What are you writing?"

She startles, her shoulders tightening. "Oh—nothing. Just some thoughts."

I lift my brow at her secrecy. She senses my lingering interest and shifts so her back is entirely to me. I pull my knees to my chest. "Meg, what are you hiding?"

The response thrown over her shoulder is so quiet I almost miss it. "Nothing, Jo. Please."

Fear drums in my chest. Mr. Brooke already made his move to wheedle into the family. He's bewitched my sister. Goodness, he's even worse than I imagined. Beth is dying and Father is bedridden and *now* is when Mr. Brooke wants to fill Meg's head with romantic nonsense.

"Meg," I say in a low voice. She hears but ignores me. "Meg!"

"*What?*"

My throat tightens. "You're writing to him, aren't you?"

"You're only a child." She sighs and continues writing. "You wouldn't understand."

Despite my efforts to keep my temper and emotions intact, tears rush to the surface. Already, so soon, so close to Beth's possible death, Meg is slipping away. "A kid. *I'm* a kid? You're the one hiding letters and keeping secrets!"

She whirls around. "Shh, you'll wake Beth."

What makes her want to leave this family so suddenly? Beth shows signs of eternal slumber and that makes Meg want to flee as soon as possible. Over the last two weeks, we have been closer than ever. We stayed up late and whispered our dreams to one another, our prayers for the higher powers to heal Beth.

Meg has been my only flame in the dark since Marmee left. She's been my anchor, and I thought I was hers.

"Go, then," I whisper when she sits beside me.

"What?"

"Go." My voice cracks. "You want to leave. If you want to break up this family and live with someone who will never understand you—never *know* you—like we do, then go. We'll be better off."

Silence festers as she considers my harsh accusation, with only the crackling of the fire between us. Outside the window, wind whistles and snowflakes tumble, uninterrupted by the storm raging on inside the March home. Frost has gathered on the sill, and I wish it would build around my heart.

Meg's soft tone cuts through the quiet. "He's been helping me through this. His letters—"

"And what have *I* been doing?" I interrupt as tears fill my eyes. "I guess we're not good enough for you anymore."

Her voice breaks. "Jo, please—"

The anger and anticipation building in my chest vanishes when Beth stirs. We lurch to our feet, for she's been sleeping without much movement for the past few days. "Go get Hannah," I order, taking Beth's hand in mine. It's less clammy than before, but I refuse to let hope blossom. The days leading to winter have not been welcoming nor joyful. The sunrise and sunsets have been less colorful, seemingly taking my advice by slowing down so Beth can catch up.

"Oh—" Hannah squeaks, a hand against Beth's head, then her neck, then her hand. She grips it tightly. "The fever's turned. Look at her. She's breathin' easy, sleepin' naturally. Oh, my goodness me."

"I'm not celebrating until Dr. Bangs looks at her."

Never before did the world seem to hold its breath. Even the wind stills; frosty branches no longer tap, tap, tap against the window. Time ticks slowly and not at all. The house sits, waits, and hopes that Beth keeps improving. A glass needle sits between my sister and me. Neither of us dares to inch closer, lest the delicate shards break into our skin.

Breaths stay nestled in our lungs as dawn approaches. Warmth begins to seep into the house unexpected and uninvited but welcomed all the same. It appears that my big heart isn't finished with me yet, for I break down into tears when Marmee arrives at last. Light and hope pour from my eyes through tears and my mouth through whispers of *thank God, I love you,* and *I missed you.* My anger at Meg for drifting from the family subsides temporarily as love fills the house in quiet, happy tears. Marmee must carry conviction and optimism on her shoulders because I've never had so much trust for a brighter future—a brighter *day.*

The sun rises in beautiful pinks and purples, seeming to blossom for Beth as she grows stronger. Mother stays by her side and tells us of Father's well-being. When she informs us that Mr. Brooke remained with him and Meg responds with "I know," the betrayal and hurt slither up my gut again. I know that we're all to leave the nest one day, but I at least thought Meg would tell me when she thought about it.

As the elder sisters, we tell each other everything—most of all our dreams and hopes. I know that she wants a house and family of her own, but it always seemed so far away and I had to hear from *Teddy* that romantic notions bubble between her and Mr. Brooke. I wanted to hear it from my sister—and even when presented with the opportunity, she called me a child and told me to mind my own business.

It's a pleasing comfort when Amy arrives home with Laurie in tow. I didn't realize how much I missed her until she croaks that I'm hugging her too tight. It's like she grew in the past two weeks, for she no longer appears as a meek thirteen-year-old, but as young woman growing into herself. She hugs and greets me with such gratitude and grace I haven't seen her don before. Nonetheless, it makes me proud.

While Hannah prepares dinner, Marmee is with Beth, and the Laurences are resting after the stressful days, I beckon Amy to sit with me on the couch. She rests in my arms and tells me about her time at Aunt March's. Laurie visited her as I had requested, and she suffered in dreadful silence without knowing Beth's true state. Guilt stabs at me for not thinking of her more often during her exile. The agony of waiting without being able to help must have been awful. But she informs me that Beth's sickness has taught her a lot about what it means to be a good, noble person.

The biggest relief of it all is that Aunt March adores her much more than she adores me. This means that Amy will be the one to tend to her. I shall miss the poky old woman, but it will grant me time to tend to Beth.

Later in the evening, as Meg writes a letter to Father—at least I *hope* it's Father—I slip upstairs into Marmee's room where Beth rests with Mother by her side. I stand in the doorway for moments, watching her hold a sleeping Beth's hand. My mother has rich, dark brown skin with hollow cheekbones and an upturned nose. Her dreadlocks twist into an elegant, plain bun at the base of her neck. Her brown eyes find mine and she holds out her hand.

"What is it, dear?"

I flinch, dropping my crossed arms and searching for my voice. "Marmee, I have something to tell you."

"About Meg?"

"How did you know?"

She tilts her head. "I knew this was coming. Come, sit, and do speak low so we don't wake Beth."

I release a sigh and settle onto the floor at her feet. My temple presses against her knee and her free hand pushes my hair back. "I hate John Brooke."

"Josephine March, don't you say such a thing," Marmee says in a sharp tone, but she manages to not sound judgmental.

"I *do*. I—"

"He has done plenty for us."

I lift my head. "Not because he truly cares, Mother. He just wants Meg. He's selfish—"

"Have you had a conversation with him—more than a few minutes?"

"Well, no, but—"

"Then how do you know his motives?"

"Because Meg is content in our family and now she wants to leave. He's done something to her. I just know it." The words sound more childish out loud, yet I can't bring myself to feel anything else.

Marmee touches my cheek. "Oh, my darling. They care for each other. That is all."

"He's going to take her away," I wail, exasperated that she isn't outraged at the idea. "He stole her glove!"

A tiny smile stretches over her full lips. "I assure you he has nothing but respectable intentions. He would like the opportunity to build a relationship with her, but your father and I refuse to consent to marriage so young."

I huff. "Meg's got a soft heart. She'll fall for anyone." Love and romance are such senseless notions. Meg acts in no such way a girl under a man's spell should act, but she's surely different. If *I'm* to have a life partner, I want none of the giggling or the blushing or the showering of romantic notions. I want him to be a friend, a companion, but someone who pushes me to be better. As of now, Meg isn't a better person.

"Jo, you will all go to homes of your own one day."

"He's not even rich," I say, trying to throw in any excuse to deter Mother from approving of John Brooke.

"Money may be good and useful, but I never wish for my girls to feel too tempted by it. Meg will possess a good man's heart, and that is better than a fortune."

I cringe. "That sounds disgusting."

Marmee sighs, glancing at Beth, then at me. "Soften your heart, my dear. It will do you good."

If John Brooke's intentions are honorable, that means he escorted Marmee to Washington out of the goodness of his heart. My family has done little to nothing to benefit him. The Laurences' help is understood—Laurie is part of the family. But John Brooke's supposed adoration for Meg is the reason for his noble deed.

For a moment, I ponder whether my irritation is birthed

from jealousy. A man wills himself to do so much for one young woman and her alone. Teddy's help is for the entire family, although I don't doubt he would run to the ends of the earth for me. I don't know. My thoughts are jumbling because I don't want Teddy in any other way than friendship. Meg tells me that our friendship isn't like any other, that many between a girl and a boy have barriers unless they're courting. Teddy and I have neither barriers nor are we courting.

As Beth gets a little stronger, Meg drifts farther from me. We hardly speak. Most of my time is spent whisking Beth around the house and ensuring she has everything she needs. In the meantime, Amy dedicates herself to donate as much of her belongings as she can. Lord only knows the real reason. When I ask her, she says, "To be noble," and moves on. We're already poor, so I fail to see the purpose, but I sit in silence and watch her empty her trunk a little more each day.

Christmastime approaches and days are supposed to be joyous, but my heart still trembles with worry about Beth and Papa. It helps to see Beth's merry face every day; she urges me to be more joyful. One evening, Teddy appears at the back door with a blanket. He drags Amy and me across the way toward his mansion. In his garden, there is a raging bonfire, bigger than I've ever seen. Beth stays home, too weak to venture into the cold, and Meg doesn't want to leave her alone.

"This isn't practical, Laurie," Amy comments, warming her hands among the flames.

"Practicality is for the wickedly boring."

I laugh. "That sounds like a famous quote."

"It should be," Teddy replies, bending down and scooping a handful of snow in his gloved hands. He molds it into a ball.

"Theodore Laurence," I warn.

Before Amy can lift her attention, a wad of snow smacks her in the face. "Oh—!"

Teddy manages to laugh and gasp at once. He covers his mouth with a hand, failing to mask his laughter. I don't even try to mask my own. "I'm so sorry," he says. "I meant to hit your shoulder!"

"Laurie! I'm not a dirty boy like you! I'm a lady!" Amy exclaims, which makes me laugh harder. I bend down and gather snow before launching it at her back. She pulls her hands from the flames and whirls toward us. "Forget it."

In an instant, we all slip into a snowball fight. During typical March sister snowball fights, we're not allowed to aim for the face since Amy used to cry every time. Tonight, she doesn't care. We throw snowball after snowball, some of them hardly even formed balls—just handfuls of snow. Sweat coats my back and my lungs ache from the frigid breeze; I don't mind. Tonight is the most fun I've had in a long time.

CHAPTER 16

FINDING HOPE

On Christmas morning, I'm the last to wake.

Amy jumps on top of me yelling *"It's Christmas!"* and drags me out of bed toward the stairs. She yanks me so hard my socks slip and almost take me to the ground.

"I'm up, I'm up."

It's a cozy morning and the aroma of Hannah's sugar cookies wafts through the house. If there's one good thing to love about Christmas, it's Hannah's famous cookies—the ones she bakes only on this day. Marmee greets me with a strong hug and a loving kiss. Meg bids me a Merry Christmas with a kiss on the cheek, but I barely give her a reaction. I gesture for Beth to stay seated on the couch and lower beside her.

"Merry Christmas, Beth."

There are few gifts exchanged this year. Last year, I said that Christmas wouldn't be the same without gifts, but Beth's health is enough of a present. I hug her a little tighter than I did yesterday.

As the morning ticks by, Teddy and Mr. Laurence make an appearance. Mr. Laurence is here for Beth; they spend most of the time at the piano together. The sight warms me. After dressing in a simple, dark purple dress that buttons up to my neck, Teddy and I sing carols to ruin the beautiful piano playing. My scratchy voice is anything but soothing. He ruffles my curly mop and earns a punch on the arm.

It doesn't take long for piano playing to tire Beth. She retires into the study to rest on Papa's couch, not wanting to venture up the stairs. The aroma of apple cider and cinnamon wafts through the house. Teddy holds mistletoe over us, causing me to throw us into a wrestling match. Amy spends half the morning getting ready; I ignore sidelong glances from Meg; the new ink Marmee bought me for Christmas presents itself in poems and quick stories. At midday, Teddy bursts into the parlor with a wild grin on his brown face. He speaks in a breathless voice.

"Here's another present for the March family."

My heart lurches at the familiar man standing in the parlor threshold.

"Papa!"

In my flurry of movement, I knock over my new ink. It spills over my short story, but I don't care. I turn it upright, wipe my inky fingers on my dress, and sprint toward my father. I hear a crash and I think Amy tripped over something. My arms secure around my father's neck and I inhale the familiar eucalyptus scent. He must have shaved recently.

A grateful sob scratches my throat because mere weeks ago, the world was caving in. Two of the most important people in my life knocked on death's door and death didn't answer. The cloud of love that occurs over the next minute passes in a blur. I don't remember Beth waking up yet her arms wrap snugly around Papa's torso. Nor do I remember Mr. Brooke walking in, but I see him *kiss* Meg! Kiss! A flush rushes over his face and he tells a blushing Meg it was an accident, but I'm no fool.

"Hey!" I march into the foyer toward him. In a flash,

Laurie's arm is around my waist and he's dragging and carrying me to the back door. "Let me go!"

"Relax, relax."

"No, I have to kick someone in the—*let me go!*"

Laurie pushes us outside and the cold air whacks me in the face. I halt on the porch and he steps down, my wrist tight in his grip.

"Come, let's walk," he says, tugging me harder.

Vexation and distress rip at my heart despite the joy surging through me moments ago. I step toward my best friend and point a finger at him. "Don't you speak the slightest of it."

He slings an arm across my shoulders. "None at all. Fresh air and the company of your boy. That is all."

If only Laurie had been quicker with matching with Meg. It's a courtship I approve of and encourage! Mr. Brooke is a stranger and I don't know his full intentions, no matter what Marmee says. I know my mother is trustworthy, but I hate the thought of anyone coming to break up this family. If Laurie and Meg married, it would be a rearrangement of the family and no one would be lost to us.

I inhale the crisp air and let my gaze roll over the brown wintry hills. With my arm around Laurie's waist, my nose and ears grow colder with each second. Peace begins to return to me once more. Until I hear Meg yelling, "Jo! Jo!" She stumbles to a stop behind us and I take my time turning around.

"Your John is waiting for you."

Her frown deepens. "Oh, please don't call him *my John*." She glances at Teddy. "Laurie, may I have a moment with my sister?"

He bows his head. "I'll be inside."

I cross my arms over my chest and don't speak until he's far enough away. "What?"

Meg's rosy cheeks redden further. The sleeves of her peach-colored dress flare around her hands as she wrings her fingers together. Her dusty brown curls blow across her face as her eyes glisten like a storm prepared to break. "I... I'm sorry."

I gulp. "For what?"

"I never wanted you to feel like I betrayed you. With Mother gone... I didn't know what to do."

"Lean on me as I lean on you," I reply. I step back and sigh to control my temper the best I can. My sister drowns helplessly and seems to ignore my extended hand. Why? Why does she ignore my support? Does she think I'm incapable of it? It wouldn't be the first task I failed at.

"I'm the oldest," Meg explains. "*I'm* the one who's supposed to offer support and guidance and I—I felt lost. And when I wrote to John about how Marmee was, because we all know she bears pain without telling us, I had a... I had someone help me learn how to keep it together—for your sake."

"Don't put this on me. I never told you to start acting like our mother." Tears fill my eyes at the excruciating memories of not knowing whether two of the most important people in my life would live to see the new year. "We *both* became Beth's caretakers and *both* carried the pain of not knowing about Papa. When Beth got sick, you bore the burden of running the house alone when I thought we shared it. Did you not think I was strong enough to do it?"

"It has nothing to do with you. Marmee told me I was in charge." She lowers her gaze and shakes her head. "You have no idea what it's like being the oldest."

All this time, Meg carried her pain with a lifted chin because Marmee wanted her to keep it together for the sake of the family. But Meg *is* part of the family; what do we do for her sake? Let her suffer?

"Even if you're the oldest and in charge, that doesn't mean you suffer alone," I explain, then remember the root of this entire situation—John Brooke. "Well, no, you didn't. You turned to a *stranger*."

"John's no stranger—*stop!*" she snaps when I scoff and begin to leave. She takes my wrist. "I'm not marrying him. Our letters were from a place of friendship, truly. There isn't a world I would pick a man over my family—over you. You're *everything* to me, Jo, and no one can ever take me from you. You have to know that!"

The reality of the future hangs between us; we're both going to leave home one day and start families of our own. I may end up an old spinster, yet one of us ends up leaving. My voice breaks and I cannot help feeling childish when I say, "You were supposed to tell me you were growing up. I didn't even have a warning and suddenly your trunk was already packed."

Meg wraps me in her arms, her hair catching my tears. "I know, I didn't mean to. It surprised me, too." She sniffles. "I promise never to keep any more secrets."

When I pull away, I wipe my wet cheeks. "I still don't like Brooke."

Meg smiles as if she expected me to say that. She grazes a thumb under my eye. "You will. Besides, there is nothing to fuss over, dear. I much agree with Mother and Father that I am too young for such things and I plan on telling him that quite soon."

I almost feel like Marmee, struggling to let her children grow up. Teddy once told me I would make a reckless mother, to which I agree. Now I fear I may end up too careful of a mother and encourage my children to live at home with me forever.

With my and Meg's relationship healed, we get to enjoy Christmas with our father. He spins tales of the war for us with Beth perched on his knee. Such love fills the house and over-flows through the windows and doors. A year ago, I was a soldier in socks, traveling through the battlefield behind Papa. Now, I warm my feet by the fire and listen to his deep, silky voice, watching him scratch his silver beard.

He makes sure to say how proud he is of each one of us. Amy, more selfless and dutiful. Meg, grown and willing. Beth, safe and a little less shy. And me, a little less wily, a little more mature, but my passion all the same.

It's a loving Christmas as are the following days. Gratitude rushes through me every morning when I see my father enjoying a cup of coffee in his usual chair. I make sure to kiss him each time—a small action I didn't realize how much I missed doing.

On the first day of the new year, Meg plans on informing John Brooke of her stance on love and romance. I watch her prance about the parlor, her chin high and her hands knotted behind her back as she recites her speech.

"Do speak quickly, though. Aunt March will be visiting soon, I believe," I remind her as I step to answer the door. For the first time in months, I don't greet Mr. Brooke with a stern glare, but with a smug smile. "Do come in, Mr. Brooke."

I wiggle my brows at Meg before dashing upstairs. Amy is in our bedroom sketching the fireplace, scolding me when I flop onto the bed. I crawl up beside her and rest my cheek on her arm.

"You're really good, Ames."

"I know," she says, elbowing my face away since I leaned on her drawing arm. "Aunt March has set up art lessons for me and I've already improved tremendously."

I gasp. "Oh, how rich! I can already see it now—*Amy Curtis March is the subject of tonight's gallery!*"

She fights to keep her gaze focused, but a smile creeps onto her lips. Such talent at only thirteen is bound to take her places and make her the golden child she constantly claims to be.

Almost everything about Amy is gold—golden brown skin, honey-gold curls, and status as the golden child.

After about ten minutes, I leave Amy to her sketching to slip downstairs. Giddiness runs up my spine at the gossiping I'm about to do. "Meg! How did he take—oh, dammit."

Except Meg isn't sitting on the couch—she's sitting on Mr. Brooke's lap in the most submissive of ways. She lurches to her feet with color rushing into her cheeks. My hands curl into fists, more out of trying to control my temper rather than preparing to sock Mr. Brooke in the face. Even though it is part of my many desires. With my eyes on him, I yell, "*Marmee!*"

"Sister Jo!" Mr. Brooke exclaims, grabbing my arms and pecking my cheek. "Congratulate us!" Then he wraps his arms around me in a tight squeeze.

My body tenses into an iron rod as dozens of ways to punish this man sprint through my mind. My eyes widen enough they're about to fall out of my head. Disgust paints my face.

"Oh—John, don't," Meg warns, placing a hand on his back. "She doesn't like hugs."

She doesn't clarify that I *do* like hugs—just on my own terms and not from a man I dislike. My cheek still tingles from his kiss. I want to gag.

"Somebody—*anybody!*" I shout, my voice cracking as I stare at the jovial man before me. He's always been calm and collected; I've never seen him smile before today. "John Brooke is acting weird... and Meg likes it!" I wipe my palm on my cheek in the roughest of ways, willing away the feeling of the kiss with my calloused hand. "I will cut off your lips if you ever kiss me again."

Still, no one arrives. I rush to the stairs and screech at the top of my lungs. "*MARMEE! PAPA!*"

The afternoon offers no such solace. My parents, Meg, and Mr. Brooke disappear into the private study for hours.

Throwing myself upon the bed in my room and wailing the awful news to Beth and Amy does no such help.

"I think it's romantic," Amy muses, crossing her legs.

"That's precisely the problem!"

Beth lowers herself onto the foot of my and Meg's bed. "What is your opposition to romance?"

"It makes girls do stupid things and turns them into fools—"

"Not if it's done right," Amy interrupts.

"*And*," I continue, "everyone treats it as if it's a girl's only passion or destiny."

"The people whose opinions matter to us don't believe that," Beth argues, tightening the red wrapper Marmee gifted her for Christmas. Perhaps she's right, but romance still has too much space in our everyday lives. Meg told me no one can ever take her from me and Marmee told me to soften my heart. Considering Amy and Beth don't agree with me and offer no comfort, I disappear into the garret for days. My footsteps creak, creak, creak, over the floorboards as I pace.

Mother and Father will give Mr. Brooke three years before allowing consent to marry. I, for one, think it should be Meg's decision, but she *agrees* with their decision. Yet my dear sister has been a follower all of her life.

I search for hope and soften my heart between the letters inked in my stories. Thus far in my life, stories have influenced, guided, and comforted me. It's time I turn back to it and discover the underbelly of my heart, for I know there is more to encounter.

CHAPTER 17

SENTIMENTAL DEEDS

THREE YEARS LATER

With my hair long and soul mended, I've begun turning into the esteemed author I have always wanted to be. The war is over and love has won. Peace flows within the March house through consistent kisses and declarations of gratitude. Despite the colorful flowers loyally spurting around the home every spring, dark days indeed pass through.

Papa and I find ourselves in scrapes and rows since I oppose his traditional beliefs of a woman's role. He wonders how I became to behave in such a way and Marmee often comes to my defense. While Meg usually agrees with me, she steps out of every argument and wishes for tranquility to reign. The rows never leave scars, but cuts and bruises of the soul that heal overnight or sometimes over a cup of tea and a hearty kiss on the cheek.

One evening, when the winter chill continues to cling onto spring nights, Papa stares into the fire with a distant gaze. Meg is teaching me to improve my sewing.

"Father," I say, "you've been staring at the fire for almost an hour. Is everything okay?"

He sighs but gives a little grin when Beth's worried eyes find his. "Quite all right, dear. I'm thinking about a sinner who confessed to me today. My heart just aches for him so; he's got demons he doesn't know how to rid."

"Maybe we can help," Beth quirks.

Father pats her hand. "No, my love. This man has confidence I should not share his wrongdoings and I don't plan on betraying him." He taps her forehead with a gentle finger. "Even though I know what's in that brain could be of use."

Over time, as I begin to loosen the reins on Meg and soften my heart, my tongue and the flame in my chest become more controllable. While I have many opinions regarding Father's daily work with religion, it is much easier to remain silent. I would find it irksome if another has negative opinions about my writing each time I bring it up—which is often, considering I write for *The Spread Eagle* on a regular basis.

Teddy has since forgotten our kiss, which I am ever so grateful for. He succeeds in college with academics yet fails to hide his mischievous deeds. While I can never have too much hope and expectations for boys, he is on the right path toward growing into the lovely young man I know he can be. And he dawdles far too much and doesn't take advantage of the wealthy resources his position grants him, I silence my lectures when he visits, for I know he receives enough scolding from Mr. Laurence and because I've missed my boy too much to lower his spirits during his short visits. My childish tendencies surface when he's around; he reminds me of a simpler time when my dreams had no obligation.

He brings his closest college friends home during the summer and winter, the ones whose personalities explain why my boy has been so rebellious. After weeks of activities with his friends, Amy and I prepare to depart for a gathering before they return to their corners of the world tomorrow.

"I don't see how you order them around in such a manner," Beth tells Amy while peeling oranges at the kitchen table. It's an unusually warm day in winter, so the window behind Beth is open. Yellow birds land on the sill to create a pleasant sight of undisturbed peace.

Amy slips on her shoes. "If you believe yourself to be of utmost importance and treat yourself that way, others will too. Eventually."

"It's all a waste of time, in my opinion," Meg perks while rolling out dough. Flour stains her rosy cheek.

I roll my eyes and continue filling the basket with the cookies I begged Hannah to bake last night. "Not all of us have a man working diligently to provide for a home that's not yet in existence. We're still enjoying our freedom."

Meg puffs. "Marriage is no prison, Jo."

"I disagree."

Amy rises and twirls, her skirt billowing around her with the haughty air of a fifteen-year-old. "*I* think marriage is like jewelry. We all want the ones worth the most money."

"Marriage is about *love*, Amy. And Jo, if marriage is done right, it is the opposite of a prison. It should make you feel more like yourself than you've ever been."

I snort at Meg's wisdom. "Marmee's lessons have been paying off."

When Amy and I enter the Laurence mansion and make our way to the parlor, I pull us aside at the sound of them gossiping about us. I clap my hand over her mouth before she can protest.

"Shh, they're talking about us," I whisper.

"It's not ladylike to eavesdrop!" But despite Amy's wish of being prim, her curiosity gets the best of her and she huddles closer.

"Your dear friend, Laurie," says Parker. "The tall one."

"Ah, yes! That's my Jo," says Teddy in a proud tone. I gape at Parker's failure to remember my name considering I've been around him for three weeks.

"What makes her the way she is?"

My chest tightens. If he should insult me, how would my boy react? Teddy's hesitant voice says, "I don't follow."

"So, gentleman-like. She's not at all like her sister, the one who I'm sure wears a crown only worthy men can see."

Amy smiles and tosses her head at the accurate description. I roll my eyes. Great. She already has a big enough ego. A maid passes, slowing at the sight of our snooping. I press my finger to my lips while Amy shoos her down the hallway.

"I understand," Teddy replies. "Jo is—set in her ways. She knows what she wants and doesn't care if it suits anyone's pleasure, for she lives for her own. Are you telling me you don't like her?"

"No, I'm not saying that at all!" Parker exclaims, which makes my eyes widen with surprise. "In fact, I like her very much. I see her as one of the boys, but I don't believe she will ever be the type of lady a fellow will fall in love with—certainly not *marry*."

I thrust the basket into Amy's arms and saunter into the room, my chin high and hands behind my back. The young men jump at my entrance; I ignore their shock and say, "I should believe that to be an asset to my personality, Parker. It drives away unworthy matches and encourages likely partnerships."

Parker laughs and hands me a genuine grin. "I believe it does, Jo!"

"And I assure you that, like my snow maiden of a sister," I add, glancing back at Amy as she sets the basket on a table and smiles at me, "I, too, wear a crown of my own that only worthy men can see. There is one reason you were unaware of that."

Teddy stares at me with pride in his dark eyes. His friends

chuckle and Parker bows his head with a hand to his heart and says, "I concede."

I plop into a reading chair. "No need, my friend. No need."

June blooms warm hearts and giddy demeanors. I dare say that the house Mr. Brooke purchased for Meg is a lovely little kingdom he named Dovecote. Meg's plain excitement is the biggest consolation of her leaving the family.

Once they started planning the wedding, Meg often spoke in private with John as he ventured back and forth between his family and here. She remained secretive about what his family is like, citing that her husband-to-be wishes the situation to stay as private as possible, though I suspect she speaks to Marmee on the matter. I don't know much, only that tension exists between John and his family, likely because he doesn't follow all of the Wampanoag customs. Meg told us she and John will be incorporating certain traditions in the wedding and that his parents would attend, but no one else from his home. My heart softens ever so slightly for him. It cannot be easy for your beloved family to abandon you on what should be a happy day.

For weeks, she and John sit alone in Papa's study making gifts. Meg says it's his people's tradition for the bride and groom to create presents for the guests. The long-awaited wedding day turns the world into sentimental beings. Aside from me, of course.

My darling sister has worked tirelessly over her wedding dress, ensuring that every stitch and every lace find a perfect home for her perfect day. Meg is a rose at the height of her bloom. I sit back, not helping her prepare, and watch her in awe for a little while. It scandalized Aunt March when my older sister declared wanting an unfashionable wedding with none but loved ones around. It tells me that John Brooke may be a lovely match for her after all; she lets the desire for love trump the desire for a haughty appearance. Her brown skin glimmers with a constant blush only true love can create. We braided her tight curls into a beautiful style behind her head, decorated with flowers she calls lily of the valley. She says they're John's favorite.

Amy hesitates to hug her in fear of rumpling the dress, but Meg pulls her into a tight embrace and says, "Wrinkle the dress, ruffle my hair. It shows the amount of love present on this day."

I watch her gather Amy and Beth into her arms and I recognize the girlish tendencies from our childhood. While Amy is in the process of leaving her youngest adolescence at sixteen, we used to ignore appearance and propriety before we reached double-digits in our age.

Meg's gaze finds mine. She announces she's going to tie John's cravat, but asks me to walk with her into the hallway. My fingers toy with the rose behind my ear—the one Marmee had picked and instructed me to put in Teddy's breast pocket.

"I'm so proud of you," I say once we're out of earshot, though I don't doubt that Amy and Beth have their ears pressed against the door. "You've worked so hard on your dress and you look like a rose in the height of bloom."

"That sounds beautiful and poetic. Do write it down for me... But is that all that's on your mind?"

I take her hands and shake my head. "No. It is a happy day, a lovely day, and I don't wish to ruin it for you. I will ask you of this one thing and then pack it away forever."

"Tell me, dear."

"I ask that you please assure me of my place in your heart."

A sad smile tugs at her lips as light seeps through the open door of Marmee and Papa's bedroom behind her. She holds my hands tighter and says, "Jo March, you are my sister, my best friend, and my home. You can never leave my heart and John Brooke will never take your place." She pokes my nose. "I'm a March first."

I throw my arms around her and fight to keep myself sober. She pulls from the hug and reveals a bracelet she'd hidden within her dress.

"John and I are supposed to give this to you together, but you're quite special," Meg says, taking my wrist and sliding on a beaded bracelet. Its purple-and-white shades don't match my dress.

I twirl the delicate jewelry. "You made this?"

"A wedding gift. One of the traditions." She leans forward and kisses my cheek. "I love you, Jo."

I pull my shoulders back and inhale. "I love you too."

When Meg vanishes to find Papa and John, I hide in the pantry for a few private moments to remind myself of the good to come and stop myself from getting caught up in the blissful past.

Marmee pressured me into wearing her old dress in the shade of burnt orange. It isn't the color I dislike; it's the ruffled short sleeves and the low neckline—a symbol of femininity and adulthood. I'm not used to it. In protest, my hair is in a long braid down my back rather than in a proper updo. Meg, in a cloud of romance and easygoing nature, has no issue.

"Hannah told me you were hiding out in here," Teddy says, closing the door behind him. "What are you doing?"

I lift my head and will the tears away. The day's light leaks through the small pantry window. "It's a wedding—but it also feels like a funeral. In a way."

He slides his hands into his pockets, his lanky body arching as he watches me. "Meg is happy."

"My sister is happy," I echo in a whisper. "I know that. But I should feel slighted I'm not part of it."

He steps closer with tranquility clouding around him. "Quite the contrary. Your approval is part of her happiness."

"A lovely consolation, I guess."

Teddy gives a soft smile. "Never fret, my Jo. I'm always going to stand by you so you'll never feel alone for the rest of your days."

I press a hand to his arm. "I'm ever so grateful for your friendship, Teddy."

He looks at my wrist and places his own beside it to reveal a similar bracelet. "We match."

A small grin hovers my lips. "Mr. Brooke made that for you?"

He nods and sobers up, clearing his throat. "Yes..."

I tuck a stray curl behind my ear, forgetting that I'd stuck a flower there. "Oh—I meant to give this to you earlier," I say, taking and stuffing it in his breast pocket.

His gaze lingers on the rose before he changes the subject. "I think that, uh—little Parker is growing desperate about Amy. He talks of her constantly, writes poetry, and moons about in a most suspicious manner. He'd better nip his little passion in the bud, hadn't he?"

The thought of someone coming to take Amy away exhausts me. I groan. "Yes, he better. We don't need any more marrying in this family for many years."

"Do be calm," he says with a chuckle. "You'll go next."

The words sound like threats seasoned with the spices around us. I toss my head. "Oh, don't fill my mind with such notions. No one wants me and every family must have an old maid. I guess it shall be me."

"Is that what you want?" he asks.

"It doesn't matter what I want. I made my bed."

My hot-tempered adolescence has branded me for life. Everyone knows of me as the hotheaded, stubborn sister. Despite my telling Parker last year that it drives away unworthy suitors, I soon realized it drives away just about all of them. Perhaps it is for the better and I'm not destined to be tethered to another forever.

"Oh, Jo," Teddy croons, stepping even closer. "You won't give anyone a chance. You have a soft side and hate letting anyone see it. If they do, you throw cold water and get so thorny everyone is scared to look at you."

"I'm the scary sister. I've accepted that. And I don't like thinking of this sort of thing. I'm far too busy to be worried about this nonsense."

He scoffs. "It's always nonsense to you."

"What else is it supposed to be?" I ask fiercely. But I collect myself as fast as I can. This day is about Meg, not me. "Look, I don't want to get cross, so let's—"

Like before, like the first blasted time I swore he'd forgotten about, my heart flies into my throat as Teddy's lips cover mine. His hand presses into my back, but my arms remain crossed. For a moment, a mere moment, I let myself indulge the possibility that the loving partner I want to be tethered to for the rest of my life is Teddy. But, exactly like the first time, the flame dies right away. The curve of his lips sliding over mine, his nose brushing my cheek, the firmness of his body against mine—it does nothing to me.

I turn away and step back into the shelves of spices. Guilt shudders through me because I'll have to kill his hope again. It feels wrong for Teddy to put me in this position. We have never explicitly spoken of our feelings, or lack of, for each other, yet I thought I'd made myself clear years ago. I don't want to break his heart. I don't want to be the cause of any pain. And I cannot let him wallow in my rejection on Meg's happy day.

"Meg and John are getting married," I whisper, my eyes stuck on the rose. Maybe he believed that to be a romantic hint.

His voice comes out as hushed as mine. "I know that."

"Weddings—they're turning everyone's head. They make everyone talk of lovers."

"Jo—"

"You'll feel different tomorrow," I insist while shifting closer to the door.

"I won't—"

"The wedding has given everyone sentimental emotions." My voice rises with firmness despite my aching soul. I want to love him. More than anything, *I want to love him.* But I don't. "I shall keep my head on straight and never forget our friendship. I suggest you do the same for a peaceful life together."

As I leave the pantry and walk farther from him, anger rises in my chest. How could he do this on such a day? It is *Meg's* day. It's all about her, and Teddy makes it about us. I tamper down the irritation, for I spoke the truth. The wedding makes everyone's heads turn to lovers and sentiment. Amy speaks to Beth about what her dream wedding will look like.

The day fills with such casual love and beauty. Beth gossips to me that Aunt March nearly has a heart attack when Meg sprints to greet our aunt with her dress flying behind her and white flowers escaping her hair.

A stunning rendition of family occurs on this day. John Brooke approaches me in private with a wish of my blessing for this marriage. Despite knowing that this wedding continues without regard for my approval, the question comforts me. My fragile emotions threaten to rise into tears; I shove them down in exchange for a stern gesture. Raising my chin, I declare my blessing in a firm voice. There is no doubt that Meg put him up to this, but I've no objection. We shake hands in what Papa calls a "manly fashion," but the formality of the gesture pings my heart with guilt. Before I know it, my sisterly side takes over and I throw my arms around him. He laughs and hugs me back.

"Her happiness is yours to keep, John Brooke. Never forget the honor you are granted on this day."

He speaks in his usual soft and inviting voice. "I promise I shall never forget."

CHAPTER 18

LITERARY SUCCESS

For Meg—

A rosy lady so loved
by moonlight and sun
calling forth passion from a
steadfast bosom in a world so
blue from hate. Oh, dear sister—
do call upon your roots so often.
A healthy soul is made joyful by
families so cozy in life with
no love of frivolous deeds
known to rot stunning gardens.

Meg cries when I gift her the poem she asked I write for her. It's a piece I'm proud of and plan to submit for publication. It seems the family jumps into spirals of our true passions as the days arrive. Teddy has gone to travel before his third year of college begins. Amy throws herself into passionate artwork in every form she can lay her hands on.

She often arrives home from Aunt March's with paint or charcoal on her hands and fingers and grows red every time I point it out, even though I mention it with the utmost praise. It declares the intensity of her dedication—a fact that should be celebrated.

The house struggles to adjust to the absence of Meg even though she lives but a short walk away. With her and Teddy gone from my everyday life, the months do not treat me as poorly as expected. My heart has more room for writing and it teaches me how to stand on my own. Rather than sharing secrets with Meg at midnight, I spend time with my pen and ink. It holds a story of my sorrow—a moment of peace where I come to terms with my maturity. I permit myself to age, and I realize my lack of doing so has been suffocating me for years.

My wily nature has yet to calm and my status as the outspoken sister remains. I no longer stir trouble for trouble's sake, but speak what I believe. I don't shy away from being wrong; I invite lessons so I can learn my way more efficiently than before. In certain settings, I struggle to hold my tongue. Most settings, truly. Marmee says I speak the truth even if it hurts others or even myself. Which results in Aunt March selecting Amy to go to Europe over me. I thought I would grow and mature above it, but a fiery fist tightens around my chest.

"Europe? *Amy?*" I sputter, pacing in and out the stream of sunlight pouring through my bedroom window. "But Aunt March said *I* would go. Why would she—"

"During your calls last month," Marmee begins, "you said that you hate the French language—and you exhibited hatred for other characteristics a traveler should have."

After a moment of digging up the memory, I groan and flop my arms. "So—my tongue. My abominable tongue has ruined me again! *A-gain!* And now Amy—who gets *everything*—is going to Europe. And I'm not."

Marmee watches me with calm, patient eyes from my bed. "She's going for her art lessons."

"And what about my writing?" My socks scrape against the linen rug with each turn. My stomach clenches as I mourn the loss of memories yet made. "Europe was supposed to inspire my next book! I would go to museums and I was—"

"When you become a famous author, you can get yourself to Europe."

A scoff escapes my lips. "I work for the same thing that just —gets *handed* to Amy? Great."

My mother purses her lips and looks down. The sight makes my emotions break apart to reveal my common sense. Of course Amy works hard. She draws and paints as much as I write—and puts up with Aunt March in the meantime. "An angel," Aunt March often calls her. A beauty of honey curls and blue eyes— characteristics from our dear father—with brown skin and a wide nose, pieces from our mother who says they honor ancestors from a faraway place in Africa. She gathers pieces of our ancestry and wields them most elegantly. Amy is a better fit for Europe.

I sigh and plop beside Marmee. She must notice my realization because she asks, "Feel better?"

I choke out a laugh and rest my head on her shoulder. "Amy is the most elegant of us all. I suppose she's the right choice."

Mother lifts a hand to my cheek and speaks softly. "A better opportunity will come." She kisses my head. "I know it."

AMY'S RECENT ART BLUNDER IS ANYTHING BUT ANGELIC and lifts my spirits in the wake of learning I won't be going to Europe. In her flurry of experimenting with art forms, she stuffed her foot in a pan full of plaster and found herself unable to get it out. Her clobbering around the house in ungraceful stomps and cries turned me into the deepest laughing fit I'd ever encountered. My stomach ached, my vision blurred, and I laughed so hard I couldn't breathe. I was far too caught in my amusement to cut out her foot, so Beth did. Beth, who gave a mere chuckle, sobered when realizing how panicked Amy was.

One day, Amy shouts for me from the bottom of the garret steps, despite my cylinder-shaped pillow—which I call my sausage pillow—lying flat on the couch downstairs. Everyone knows that my flat pillow means *stay away*. It interrupts my writing flow and makes me tumble from the peak of the story I'm writing. With a loud groan, I stomp into the parlor.

Amy spills her plan to invite a bunch of girls over to the house since their drawing class will be ending soon. It sounds expensive and too much effort for haughty people.

I cross my arms. "Why in the world would you spend your money, worry the family, and turn the house inside out for a group of girls who don't give a hoot about you?" I grab my sausage pillow, prepared to whack her with it. "I thought you had too much pride and sense to entertain a mortal woman just because she wears French boots and rides in a *coupé*."

Amy catches my sausage pillow and sends me a stern glare. "Oh, shut it, Jo. I hate being patronized as much as you do. The girls do care for me and I for them and they have a great deal of kindness. Just because you don't care to make people like you and go into society as if they all owe you something doesn't mean that's what I do."

"The only thing I'm *owed* is silence when my sausage pillow is flat."

She rolls her eyes and tosses it onto the couch. "Will you help me or not?"

I shake off my irritation because the story I was writing wasn't flowing well, anyway. "Fine," I huff, and the day very much turns into a disaster. I sail about as a soldier under her demand, but her plan unravels idea by idea. Alas, I shall leave it up to her to tell the tale of her dreadful occurrence, for I cannot accurately depict her silent sadness in which I know her thoughts spiral.

My spirits lift highest when my passion for writing holds me in its grip—even though I'm sleepy, exhausted, and moody. This wave of dedication shines through dozens of short stories, poetry, and the progress of my novel. My scribbling suit consists of a woolen pinafore that I am free to wipe my pen on and a cap that gathers my curls for hours at a time with a bright red bow adorning the top. After two weeks, I flee from my writing vortex to escort a family friend, Miss Crocker, to a lecture about the pyramids in Egypt. I only accepted to take her because Marmee begged me to get out of the house and enjoy the fresh air. The lecture topic doesn't generally interest me, but it may hold inspiration for stories to come.

I wear a vest over a blouse, paired with a blue skirt. My hair, bundled in my usual newsboy cap, hasn't been washed in over a week. The attendees of the lecture interest me because I adore watching people and studying their interactions with others. It helps with writing realistic characters.

Miss Crocker is an old lady pushing eighty years old. I'm not sure why she wants to be here, considering her hearing isn't very good. When we take our seats, a young fellow with small feet and hands is lost in whatever he's reading in the newspaper. My gaze stretches over the paper at what looks like a fiction story.

He finishes reading and catches me as I stare. "Want to read? It's a really good story."

I accept the paper with a smile and drag my eyes over the words of love, mystery, and murder. In all honesty, it's a treacherous story. The plot jumps back and forth, which is confusing for readers, the clothing descriptions are misplaced, the character representation is off, and the relationships are horribly written.

The boy next to me rambles about his adoration for the story and the author. I don't pay much attention until he points to the unrecognizable name at the bottom of the page.

"Do you know her?" I ask.

"No, but I know she makes a good living out of these stories."

I smother my perked attention, but eagerness slips into my tone. "Truly?"

"Oh, yes! A friend of mine who works for this paper told me. The writer knows just want people want—and writes it."

A giddy sensation runs up my spine as the lecture begins. I planned on paying attention, but I lose myself in thought for the next hour. For such a time, I was content with spinning nonsensical romances for *The Spread Eagle*, believing it's what everyone wants to read. The world obsesses over love, but this writer is proof they crave more of something I can relate to. While I'm no murder detective, I wish to read those stories and it seems others do as well!

I jump into work as soon as I get home. Plotting, outlining, jotting down ideas. The story begins in Lisbon, and I use the descriptions Teddy wrote me from his travels as inspiration. A murderer targets a famous family and wants to assassinate them one by one; the killer leaves clues and it's up to the main character—a member of the family—to discover who it is before her relatives are killed. It takes weeks to write this manuscript. I obsess over every dialogue, description, and plot point.

I send away my polished story with trembling hands. Since Teddy is away at college, I can't confide in him. The wait is long, lonely, and painful. I question my worth and skill as a writer each day.

The one pleasant distraction is when Meg tells me she's with child and that I'm going to be an auntie! She announces it to the family not long before my twentieth birthday since her belly has grown much too noticeable to hide. Although I cannot imagine the discomfort of something growing inside of you, it comforts me to see Meg letting herself relax as John cares for her. He rubs her feet, makes her dinner, and even combs her hair.

But then I begin to worry about my story again, for it won't unburden my mind longer than an hour each day.

As hope begins to slip, a letter arrives. *The* letter. When I open the envelope, a check for one hundred dollars falls into my lap, but I don't focus on that. The editor praises my work and skill as a literary masterpiece and one of the best stories he has ever read. His kindness snakes through the paper and latches onto my heart. Tears drip from my eyes and I can only sit there for five minutes in a puddle of gratitude and joy.

When I regain my sense, I rush into the parlor and beckon Marmee, Papa, Beth, and Amy near. They exude joy and pride at my success and adore the little story I wrote. Papa praises specific aspects of my work, but I can see hesitation flickering in his blue eyes.

"What is it?"

He sighs, and Marmee's shoulders droop as if preparing for an argument. But I'm much too happy and proud of myself to let anything bring me down.

"Don't misunderstand," he begins, "it's a beautiful story. Well written and developed. I know that you can do better, Jo. You write *strong* stories. Do not dim your light if the world can't handle it."

I indeed wrote this story from the simple fact that it's what the world wants to read. But I also enjoyed writing this piece because it differed from the nonsensical love tales I'd written for so long. "Father, I'm still learning my way."

"I know, dear." He kisses my forehead. "And for that, I'm endlessly proud of you."

"*I* think the money is the best part," Amy muses, staring at the check with big eyes. "What will you do with such a fortune?"

"Send Beth and Mother to the seaside for a month or two."

The two of them protest right away—which I expected. I already rallied my stubbornness and win the debate in less than a minute. To the seaside they go and while Beth doesn't improve as much as I wish, Marmee is rejuvenated. It pleases me to see my money put to good use for the people I care about. The feeling is strong enough that I begin to write more and more.

It's a relief to be writing as a job. Soon, I will obtain enough status and respect to write only the stories of my heart. Beth is healthy, Meg and the baby are healthy, Amy is improving, and, as far as I know, Teddy succeeds in his educational endeavors. We write often, but he tells me very little about his academics. He asks about the well-being of Amy, Beth, Meg, and the family. His letters are short and I ponder whether he's angry at me. I pray that he's moved on from the kiss—again. It's best that he's at college. Distance ought to mend a broken heart, right?

A cloud hovers my heart at the thought of causing him any kind of pain, for I've only ever tried to help him. It is a burden to hold someone's heart, and a dangerous task at that, equipped to ruin lives and friendships. I don't tell him about my literary successes. It's too grand to be told over a letter and I will surprise him when he returns home.

My family and I debate whether I ought to do as the publisher requests for my novel. Meg protests my cutting and chopping because she believes it's perfect the way it is. Amy is logical and practical, ordering me to do what I must for success.

I confess that I let the rewards get to my head, but the results make up for such a moral sacrifice. My stories pay for the groceries, new carpets, and new clothes for the growing Meg. Alongside these little tales, I work on my novel. This idea has been cultivating for years and is the first one I had after Amy burned my first book. It is about a recent widow named Nancy and a lawyer named Augustus. When Nancy is falsely accused of murdering her husband, Augustus is supposed to prosecute her. His bosses order him to do his job, but he doesn't believe she's guilty. Nancy, Augustus, and Nancy's best friend, Grace, run a rogue investigation to determine the killer before the killer gets them.

"Jo, I don't like you writing such morbid stories," Papa says from his usual chair before the fireplace.

"Not to worry, Papa. I have plenty of story ideas about life and love, with no hint of the morbidness you despise. And this is not as morbid as you think. It's a story about morality, love, and the complexities of human nature. It presents the beauty of being peaceful and the ugly of being hateful."

Meg, lounging on the couch rubbing her swollen belly, nods and says, "She's right. It's not the kind of story I usually like, but it's one of the best novels I've ever read. It's less eerie and sinister than I thought it would be."

Papa sighs and loses himself in thoughtful consideration. For a reason I have yet to decipher, I settle on a decision when Beth says, "I should like to see it printed soon." A sense of urgency flares inside me and I begin the chopping process—for Beth's sake. It hurts, for it feels like I'm cutting up my insides, but one look at my sister's proud face and I'm back to cutting.

Meg admires the tragedy, so I dump in more. Amy objects to all of the fun, so I carve it out. After thinning the book by one-third in two weeks of nonstop work, I send it out into the scary world.

And so the new year joins us, my book is printed and praised and criticized, and I receive three hundred dollars. During the process a heavy rock settles in my gut. I took the book of my heart and turned it into a piece of literature I don't recognize.

CHAPTER 19

PASSION AND POSSIBILITIES

When June arrives and Meg gives birth, Marmee walks out of the bedroom and says the new mother had twins! My stomach could not stand being in the room during the birth; my sister's agony rattled me and Marmee cast me out because I was not of much use.

I sit beside Meg's bed as she cradles both babies. The glowing mama and her healthy babies, a boy and a girl, are a beautiful sight to behold. "Hi," I whisper, pushing aside the blanket to reveal the boy baby's face. "I'm your uncle Jo."

Meg gives me a quizzical look. "Uncle?"

"Who says it must be so divided? They may call me what they please. Joey, even. As long as they are happy."

Days after the birth, when Teddy finally comes home, he sneaks into the kitchen of Dovecote with a mischievous smirk. I gasp and drop the corn I'm husking at the table as he whispers, "How's the little mama?"

Hannah flinches and drops the saucepan, the loud *bang* echoing. We laugh and I fly ahead to throw my arms around his neck in a grateful embrace.

"You're back!"

He laughs a hearty laugh and hugs me so snugly that we lose balance and stumble. "I missed you, too, little writer. Why didn't anyone tell me Meg gave birth before I came home?"

I pull away and grip his shoulders. "We wanted to surprise you. I have *so* many surprises for you!"

"I can't wait to learn about it," he says with a grin stretching over his handsome brown face as I drag him toward the stairs.

I guide him into the nursery where Meg rocks one of the twins and John rocks the other. Teddy's eyes brighten at the sight of John. He walks closer and pushes aside the blanket to gush over the cute little face.

"Teddy," I say, tapping his shoulder.

He turns around and I point to Meg, and he does a quick double-take. "By Jupiter! Twins!"

The hours are filled with a joyful, merry homecoming. Teddy spills tales of the school year, including his many encounters with trouble. He nearly trips with excitement when I show him my published novel. A dimness hovers over my heart when I give it to him, for I know I'm not completely proud of it.

I smother the hesitation in the trailing days by helping Amy at her art fair, where her talent ought to speak for itself. Her table is filled with an array of masterpieces and the most famous artists should fear my baby sister. One day, she'll steal their glory—and rightfully so.

Except everything goes wrong when Miss Chester, the woman who runs the art show, changes her table placement to a spot in the corner—a route that very few shoppers pass through! When Amy comes to me with tears brimming her eyes, I have to contain my temper so I won't lash out and hurt someone.

Amy cries that Miss Chester believes we gossiped in a poor manner about the Lambs. My sister scolds and reprimands me, for I made a fleeting joke last month when I accompanied her on calls. Marmee and I try to mend the situation to no avail.

"Don't back down," I order with a hand on her shoulder. "Stand firmly in your place even if they don't like it."

She shakes me off without regard to the stares of others. "I don't intend to be mean just because they are. I hate such childish things! It shall all work out in the end."

"I'm sorry, Amy. I'm going to make this right, okay?" I assure her as a plan already forms in my head. I enlist Teddy's help alongside his friends the next day. We'll chat with customers and direct them over to Amy's table.

"Is that my boy?" I call, leaning over the gate as Teddy advances.

"As sure as this is my girl!" He passes through the gate and takes my arm, lacing it through his as we walk inside. The side entrance leads to a long hallway, closer to where Amy's table sits.

"Where are Parker and Hayes?" I ask, glancing behind us. The sun gleams against the mahogany floors.

"They ought to be here soon."

"Ames is frantic and scared the day won't go as planned." I unhook my arm from his and squeeze his shoulder. "Do go find them and I will thank you forever."

Teddy takes me by the waist and backs me into the wall. He leans close enough for his breath to fan my face.

"Couldn't you do that now?"

My chest tightens and I try to push the shock and discomfort off my face. It's clear he hasn't forgotten our kiss last year. I remove his hands and step aside. "Go away, Teddy. I'm busy."

I sift through my memories for any reason why he *still* believes I want him in that way. Fear washes over me at the conclusion that he may not be utterly out of his wits to continue his advances. During our first kiss, I pulled him toward me. He may think I said to act as though it never happened because I was frightened of Marmee's reaction. With the second kiss, I indulged him for but a moment. He may think I believed his attempts to be insincere due to the wedding. Guilt builds in my chest for feeling as though I guided him in the wrong direction. Although, I, too, have been trying to figure out where I stand with courtship and romance.

I shove aside the thoughts and pour my focus into Amy. The day passes with success, which is a perfect farewell from America before she sets to sail off to Europe. She spends days in a panic about packing the right clothes and materials, for she wants to look her best while painting among the most elite artists. The afternoon before her departure, I sit on my bed watching her fill her trunk. I tried to help but she scolded me because she wants everything placed in a certain way. But as she organizes each item, her demeanor dims a little more.

"What's wrong?" I ask, resting my temple on the bedpost.

She sighs. "Do you promise you're not upset? That I'm the one going to Europe?"

The worried furrow in her brow sends warmth through my stomach. Amy sits on the ground and, in a second, she looks like the meek little sister who always tried to be the best she could be. "I promise." I chuckle and extend my hands toward her. "You will have a grand time and I am eager for you."

She takes my hands and lowers beside me. "I'm not a fool, Jo," she says in a low voice. She angles her head, as if to lift her gaze to me but is too weak to do so. "My entire life, I thought you hated me."

"Hate you? No, I—"

She suddenly raises her eyes to mine. "And I know it's because I never suffered poverty the way you and Meg have as young children... Marmee told me."

"I—" One of my hands slides away from hers, although I'm not quite embarrassed to have possessed those emotions. It's an old, petty feeling I am glad to admit I overcame. "My behavior wasn't fair. I... I should have been happy you don't have those memories."

Amy hesitates, then tightens her fingers around mine, her shoulders hunched. "For so long, I—I never understood why our relationship was so tough. My conceited attitude did nothing to help."

My sisterly duty to encourage and comfort rushes to the surface. "You were a child," I insist, brushing away a curl from her face.

"As were you," she counters. "Before I matured, I said awful things to you. But I—I want to let you know that I don't think of you as beneath anyone because you don't meet society's expectations. They're not made for people like us, and you learned that much quicker than I."

Her proper speech, her manner laced with grace—pride swells in my chest at the sight. "I'm happy to see you accept yourself, Amy." I poke her nose—the one she used to hold much insecurity over. "*All* of you. I couldn't be more proud."

A smile hovers her face as she takes our entwined hands and holds them to her heart. "Let us cherish our past for the lessons they hold."

I squeeze her fingers. "And look to the future for beautiful possibilities."

MEG HAS A FAMILY OF HER OWN, BETH IS SATISFIED AND comfortable, and Amy is off to Europe. My sisters are following their dreams and I sit twiddling my thumbs, waiting for greatness. When I suggest going to Marmee's friend, Mrs. Kirke, as a governess, my family is surprised, but not displeased.

"Well, now that Amy's off to Europe and Meg is a mother, I

feel I ought to do something to stir the pot and help with my writing inspiration," I explain.

I confess that envy seizes my gut every time a letter from Amy arrives, but it subsides when Marmee reads them aloud. Amy flourishes in fancy settings and her accounts of the trip show no evidence of the little girl who misspells everything and holds conceit close to her heart. My little sister is growing into herself and Europe is helping her do that.

After a few weeks of planning and exchanging letters, I pack my bags and depart for New York City for the winter, eager to meet the new Jo March. Tickling anticipation flutters throughout my body the entire train ride. Tears threaten to spill as my heart already longs for the presence of my family, but an Irish lady with many rowdy little ones distracts me.

The walk to Mrs. Kirke's takes twice as long as it should; I cannot keep my eyes on the path ahead. The world whirling around me proves much more interesting. People curse and look at me funny when I bump into them as I study the tall buildings and large crowds. And this is the everyday setting! I've never seen so many people close together when not attending a party or play or another formal gathering. You don't have to own a carriage or ask someone to borrow theirs—plenty of them ride along the street and all you have to do is call for them!

My nose and ears turn numb, an easy feeling to ignore. How have I never come here before? It feels as though anything is possible; no one knows me. I don't walk through the streets as Jo March as I do in Concord. Here, my free spirit isn't a rarity. I can be whoever I want.

Mrs. Kirke welcomes me with a bright face and open arms. "Oh, hello, my dear!" she says, holding me in her arms. "By Jove, how you've grown a foot since I last saw you!"

My nerves settle at her excitement. I grin. "It's lovely to see you."

The narrow but long house has bunches of children running around. Other adults greet me with a smile or a nod. The room I'll be staying in is small and simple and more than enough to fulfill my needs. The two little girls who will be my students are Agnes and Lucy. The name Lucy reminds me of the girl Beth dreamed about when she had the scarlet fever. I shove down the painful memories and focus on the girls. Both of them remind me of Amy, as they are prim and proper with bows in their hair.

Before Mrs. Kirke leaves me alone with them, she advises I try telling them a story to break the tension. I select a tale called "The Seven Bad Pigs." The spoiled girls don't welcome my presentation at first, but their laughs encourage me when I push up my nose and speak in a nasal voice with an occasional snort. I prance around the study and they soon hop up, too, and prance with me while making snort sounds of their own. We pass the bookshelves and chalkboard, weaving between student tables and chairs.

At the end of the story, I flinch when hands begin clapping. A man leans on the threshold of the parlor. My face warms at the thought of him watching me make pig noises and jumping around the room like a child. His beard clouds his charming smile.

"That was very goot," he says, his accent thick.

I tuck a stray curl from my bun behind my ear. The little girls giggle and run up to him, trying to climb the bear of a man. He's tall and older than me—by at least a decade—with brown hair and kind eyes.

"Bhaer, Bhaer!" the girls shout.

Mr. Bhaer bends down and scoops them up, half carrying half dragging them farther into the room. The endearing sight settles peace inside me. Mrs. Kirke's boarding house has done nothing but radiate comfort thus far.

"Jo, dear!" Mrs. Kirke calls as she enters the study. "Would you like some tea—oh." She halts when seeing Mr. Bhaer and smiles. "I see you've met the professor."

"Not quite," I say.

"Well, Friedrich Bhaer, this is Jo March. She will be our new governess for little Lucy and Agnes. Jo, this is Professor Bhaer."

With one child hanging on his arm, he begins to raise the other, but Lucy latches onto it like a branch and pulls it back down. The two of us giggle and resort to head nods and soft smiles.

Teaching occupies me for the next few days. Miss Norton, a friend of Mrs. K's, takes a liking to me during her calls at the house. Most society women do not tolerate, let alone like, me, but I cannot complain, for her sweet smiles and piqued interest in me lift my spirits because I typically eat in my room. I'm much too bashful to socialize among the academics. Despite my constant reading and educating myself, my stomach twinges from feeling inadequate. One evening, when I decide to retire to the fire, the professor is already there.

"Oh—sorry."

He quickly rises from the reading chair. "No, it is goot! You may stay." He gestures toward the fire, then toward the couch. "There is plenty of room."

After an awkward moment of consideration, I lower onto the couch. During my first night in the city, I learned that it is never completely silent. The majority slumber, and the remaining pedestrians and drunken fellows outside speak louder than they ought to. I stare at the flames and fix my posture.

"Is it your first time in New York City?" says the professor.

I chuckle. "Am I that obvious?"

"You haf a curious mind." He laces his fingers together across his stomach. "I can see it in your eyes."

I'm not sure what my eyes possess that say I have a curious mind. I'm also unsure of when we've looked at each other long enough for him to study my eyes. Was he looking at me without my knowledge? Was I slouching? I shake off the insecurity and turn my attention to the professor who already watches me with engaging curiosity.

"How long have you been here?" I ask.

"Almost a year. I care for my nephews, Franz *und* Emil, because my sister wishes for them to haf an American education."

Mrs. Kirke introduced them during her brief tour of the house and its guests. The next question presses on my tongue. "Where are you from?"

"Berlin," he says, then adds, "Germany."

I offer an amused smile. "I know where Berlin is, Professor Bhaer."

He smiles in return, lowering his head. "My friends call me Fritz."

My stomach tingles. This is the first conversation I find myself in with him and now he regards me as a friend. Many of the men around here lift their noses and chins at me. It is not a far assumption that they think themselves better than me.

"I see you are a writer," Fritz says in the silence, the crackling fire accompanying the conversation.

"How—oh." I lift my ink-stained hand. "Yes. I am."

He sniffs and sits up straight. "What do you write?"

"Stories."

"Romance?"

"You believe me to write romance because I'm a woman?"

Fritz raises a brow at my sudden accusation. "I guess I should not make uh—assumptions, then."

"Never mind that," I reply, my shoulders drooping. "Because sadly, you assumed correctly."

He smiles. "Why sadly, Mees Marsch?"

The accented lilt of my name is endearing. "Please, call me Jo," I reply, my ears turning hot. He's the first stranger—outside of editors—I've spoken to about my work. He's the first *interested* stranger. "And—I would much prefer adventurous stories rather than romantic tales."

"And why do you not write what you wish?"

"Because one must write what sells, for my family must eat."

My stomach tightens when Fritz shakes his head and leans his elbows on his knees. A sudden passion washes over him. But before he can utter a word, a small voice says, *"Onkel."* A little boy in a nightgown stands in the parlor doorway, rubbing his eyes with distress on his pale face. *"Ich kann nicht schlafen."*

"Ich komme." Fritz rises and meets the boy. He tosses a look over his shoulder and flashes me a sweet smile. "We can haf this conversation another night, *ja?*"

"Ya—I—I mean... yes."

When he carries the little boy upstairs, I drop my head in my hands from both embarrassment and relief.

CHAPTER 20

AFFECTION IS FICKLE

Living in New York perks my creativity. The evenings I don't spend with the children, I stay cooped up in my bedroom and write.

One day, upon asking Mrs. K to watch the girls during lunch, I venture through the city toward *The Weekly Volcano* office, a newspaper I found upon research. The editor, Mr. Dashwood, is a relentless man who cares nothing for morality. He informs me that morals don't sell and people want entertainment. Even though the statement unsettles me, I try to regard his knowledge. He understands the writing market much better than I do. He chops and cuts my stories into unrecognizable pieces of literature and asks what name I wish to use. The question almost insults me; why should I feel proud of the trash he turned my work into? I kindly ask for anonymous credit and accept my payment.

Everyone in my family, aside from Amy, would be disappointed in me. Sensation stories with intense thrill and mystery interest me on a typical day. However, a larger lesson makes it all the more entertaining. It gathers the world's adventures and helps give life meaning. But Dashwood claims that society wants nothing but mindless entertainment and I convince myself that the money is worth it. I remind myself of the pride in my heart every time I send my family money.

In the letters I receive, Marmee begs me to give myself a pleasant birthday. I have not made friends with anyone here so I settle for a visit to the City Library on my joyous day—despite it being rather gloomy.

The rainfall taps against the tall windows in a consistent rhythm. The day's overcast darkens the library, leading to candelabras and chandeliers alight in the middle of the afternoon. Groups of people scatter among the mahogany tables and speak with bowed heads and low voices. I pass a boy sitting alone as he crinkles the pages of his book with each turn.

I scour the aisles for where I might find a copy of *Wuthering Heights* and ascend one of the ladders. A squeal escapes me when I find it, for rereading a beloved novel on my twenty-first birthday is a wonderful celebration, but the accented voice breaking the quiet startles me.

"I do not belief it's proper to stand up there, Mees Marsch." Standing below me is the professor! He watches me with a curious glint in his eyes.

"Professor Bhaer! How funny to see you here." I grin and descend the ladder. "I was looking for one of my favorite novels."

He folds his hands behind his back. "Ah. And that is?

"*Wuthering Heights,*" I say, and his expression twists. "Why such a face?"

"I haf read it many years ago. I do not remember much, only that the characters are horrible."

I sit on the ladder step and can't keep myself from diving into a rant about the book. "That's precisely why I love it. Characters in stories don't have to be pure and innocent. It's not realistic. I like Catherine and Heathcliff because they are so easy to hate. Not all stories are meant to be enjoyable. They are created to make you *feel* something, whether those feelings are good or bad."

Professor Bhaer's head remains bowed as he listens. "I suppose," he says after a moment, "but do you not think there should be something to—uh... what is the word? Redeem them? It's not easy to forgif people who have wronged you so terribly."

A memory grips me, quick and strong, and I fight the longing clench in my stomach to be with my family again. I hum as I perch my elbows on my knees, book in hand. "When I was about fifteen, my little sister—her name is Amy—was angry with me. In turn, she burned the novel I'd been writing for years."

His eyes widen. "She burned your novel? All of it?"

I revel in my lack of lingering anger. My soul has moved past it and the event makes a good tale to share in moments like these. "All of it. Years of work went up in flames within seconds —because of a small argument."

"Do you still speak with her?"

I chuckle. "Of course I do. She's my sister."

"But what she did—that is—that is most reprehensible!"

I cannot deny his statement, but the memory of Amy's crime against my work does nothing to me now. I love her more than books. I shrug while flipping through the pages of *Wuthering Heights*. "I forgave her."

He smiles incredulously. "I am astonished. Forgifness is the hardest emotion to obtain."

"Forgiveness may be the toughest emotion, but sisterly love is the strongest."

Professor Bhaer slides his hands into his pockets and leans against the bookshelves. "You're very wise, Mees Marsch. Why do you not join the conversations at *Frau* Kirke's?"

I lower my eyes from his. "I'm afraid I don't feel very

welcomed among you scholars. You have all gone to college and I haven't."

"That is your doubt talking." He shakes his head. "I know many men who haf a college education, but none are half as thoughtful or smart as you."

The praise takes hold of my heart and a bashful tinge rises to my cheeks. For moments, I'm too sheepish to reply as I search my thoughts for the proper response. I run my fingers along the braided updo at the base of my neck.

Professor Bhaer must notice my struggle. He clears his throat and asks, "Would you like to haf a cup of coffee?"

My nerves begin to fade. The aroma of coffee is the one thing this day is missing. It's not quite the birthday I imagined, but it's welcome all the same.

"Yes, I would."

When Miss Norton extends party invitations to me and the other governesses working for Mrs. K, I almost decline on the grounds I do not have a good enough dress. Miss Norton wears nothing that costs less than a hundred dollars; I have no business attending one of her gatherings.

Alas, my esteemed hostess lends me an outfit and insists I come. It's not my usual fashion—fancy frills and ruffles never are—but I cannot deny the beauty of the dress. The shade matches the sky on a cloudless, bright spring day and my hair twists into a chignon at the base of my neck. The gloves that reach my elbows keep me warm during the short walk.

The grand building the party is at has a long set of stairs to reach the front door. I tug my borrowed cape over my chest as guests curve around me and begin up the steps. A pang of longing echoes through my body; I miss Meg. She would tell me what to do and how to act. I am unworthy of attending a gathering in such a stunning place. My heart thunders as I turn my gaze down the sidewalk I'd come from. Would anyone notice if I didn't show up?

No, I must attend. I inhale, shake off the nerves, and grab the skirt of the dress to ascend toward the party. The familiar faces—the students and scholars living under Mrs. K's roof—are calming. I smile as Fritz and his nephews approach me. Franz greets me with a loud voice and throws his arms around my waist, forgoing propriety without hesitation. Meanwhile, Emil, ever the gentleman, takes my gloved hand and kisses it. I laugh.

"Mees Marsch," says Fritz, a blush coloring his cheeks, "you look... you look—goot."

With a hand on Franz's shoulder, I reply, "I told you, Fritz. Call me Jo."

I try to socialize out of respect for Miss Norton's invitation. But many of the women concern themselves with New York society—a territory I know nothing about. And the men speak of subjects I cannot follow along with nor understand no matter how hard I try. The eloquent manner in which they speak and their passion make me wish I can fathom the topics.

After a few drinks, I hang around the outskirts and lower onto a chair. My initial feeling upon arrival returns—I am too inadequate to socialize with these people. I do not wish to hang around the children all of the time; I spend enough hours with them during the day, so I sit contently. My heart aches as I reminisce about the last formal party I attended years ago—with Meg. It was the night I truly met Teddy. Both of them have tried bringing me to gatherings since then, but I refused each time. Meg would be so proud that I haven't spoiled anything. The lent gloves are clean and neat and the dress is unburned. Tears threaten my eyes. I miss my family.

"Why you are alone?" a deep, accented voice asks.

Before me, Fritz stands with a curious furrow in his brow. I attempt a smile and shove back my tears. "I'm afraid parties are not my favorite. Not always. And I'm much too stupid to understand half of the conversations about philosophy and such."

"Don't say such things!" he insists and lowers beside me despite my not inviting him. "You may learn."

"They wish for conversations, not to host lectures." I turn my gaze to him. For the first time tonight, I study his elegant appearance, which much differs from his usual tousled hair and uncombed beard. But tonight, his dark hair slicks back with grace and his neat beard is free of any tugging, an action I notice he does often. "What are you doing over here? Should you not be enjoying the party?"

He beams, lacing his fingers together. "I'm much like you, Mees Jo. I haf no wish to—uh—" He waves his hand toward the crowd as he searches for the English words. "Be around stupid people."

I laugh. "But you are with me."

"You are not stupid," he says as his eyes linger on me. It may be a German thing, but I often find him staring. "Would you like to leaf?"

I tilt my head. "I'm sorry?"

"Leaf." He waves his hands as if shooing someone away. "Go. Go home."

An inevitable smile pulls at my lips. Fritz watches me. "I would love that."

We swipe our coat and cape from the private room and dash down the hallway. Giddy smiles and chuckles pass between us as we inch toward a hallway intersection like escaping children.

"Won't it be rude?" I ask, securing my cape around my shoulders.

"There are many guests. She won't notice—*wait!*"

Fritz takes my arm and pulls me into an alcove decorated

with an old painting. Apprehension washes over me when voices echo at the hallway intersection. His hands hold my arms and we freeze, waiting for the danger to subside.

"That was close," he whispers after releasing a breath.

A giggle bubbles in my throat. After peeking into the hallway, I grab his wrist. "Let's go. Be quick!"

Fritz and I fly out of the building. He holds my hand as we rush down the stairs so I don't trip. The cold air seeps into my lungs but I expend it with each laugh and puff. The journey to the house is short and filled with recantations of the night's moments that made us want to leave in such a hasty manner.

Inside the house is considerably warmer than outside. Our mirth continues fluttering around as we shed our outer garments.

"Shh, we don't want to wake anyone," Fritz whispers, taking my hand while walking upstairs.

My dress tightens around my body and I long to shed it. We reach the point in the hallway where we mean to split toward our separate bedrooms. "That was very fun."

His dark eyes steady on me. "It was."

Tension slips between us. I peel off my gloves to distract my nerves. "Well—goodnight, Fritz."

"Uh—wait," he says when I turn to leave. "I would like to show you something."

Excitement flickers in my heart. I don't want the night to end yet, for it feels as though it has just begun. "What is it?"

"Follow."

I smother my hesitation at the blunt instruction and follow him toward his bedroom. The night's cold seeps through the windows and walls; chills shudder over my arms and I hug myself for some warmth.

Fritz walks in ahead of me. "I haf been wanting—are you cold?"

"A little."

He changes course and rushes toward the heating stove. "I shall get a fire."

I smile at his use of words—getting a fire rather than starting or making. I wander toward his bookshelves. "You have many books."

"Ah, yes." He places bits of log inside the stove. "That's what I wanted to show you. I realize we only spoke about philosophy over coffee. I still want to know about the stories you write."

My fingers run along the book spines, savoring the ridges of both beaten and new leather. "Shakespeare!" I exclaim with a gasp, sliding the book from its place.

"Yes. Do you like him?"

"I admire him very much," I whisper while flipping through the pages of *Romeo and Juliet*. When I turn, I find Fritz sitting on the ground in front of the heating stove, his arms secured around his bent knees. Such a boyish arrangement on a grown man. A smile pulls at my lips. I take the skirt of my dress and sit before him, the blue fabric spilling around me. I set down my borrowed gloves. "*Romeo and Juliet* is one of my favorite love stories."

His face dims. "It is no love story."

"Why, sure it is. They do all of it for the sake of love."

He opens his palm and I hand him the book. He skims the pages. "*Romeo and Juliet* is a tragic tale and unromantic in the clearest of ways."

I raise my brows. "Then do enlighten us lesser folk."

"I—I did not mean it in such a manner. Forgive me." Fritz stares into my eyes. "Shakespeare uses love as a weapon. They are but children and children are tempted to do the opposite of what adults say." He holds up the book. "Romeo and Juliet are fascinated with each other and the excitement of defying their families adds wood to the fire."

The heat from the stove wafts over my skin, willing away the chill. Loose strands from my updo tickle the back of my neck. "But they don't want to defy their families. They want to be happy together."

"They don't know what they want. They are *Kinder*. Children."

"I believe we ought to give them more regard for their knowledge. They all have wishes and we should acknowledge that."

Fritz nods, digesting my words. "Yes, perhaps so. But they haf the—the"—he opens and closes his fingers in a talking gesture as he searches for the English word—"voices! They haf the voices of society on their shoulders. They are young—and gifen the jobs of adults. If they should wish to be together, they ought. But Shakespeare shows the danger of gifing too much work to children. There is too much violence and expectation and they feel cornered and without hope—so they kill themselves."

Of the several times I've read *Romeo and Juliet*, Fritz's interpretation is new. He offers a way of thinking I have not yet considered. I listen to his impromptu lecture with admiration. Our refreshing conversation about literature and the power it holds brings me a sense of hope about the world. In Concord, I was alone. No one cares about literature the way I do or thinks in such a critical manner.

He lights a candle and grabs his reading spectacles to read me a scene that supports his argument. When he shifts to sit shoulder-to-shoulder with me, I can't help sneaking glances at him. It's bewitching to watch him search the pages in a spell of passion.

"Aha! Here." Fritz points to Capulet's dialogue:

My child is yet a stranger in the world;
She hath not seen the change of fourteen years. Let two
more summers wither in their pride
Ere we may think her ripe to be a bride.

A droplet of saliva flies from his lip as he speaks. The manner in which he wipes his mouth and clears his throat is anything but handsome. I am not drawn to his attractive or unattractive qualities; I am drawn to the tranquility that softens my heart when I am in his presence.

"Now, many argue with her, as you know," he continues, "and don't want to let children be children. Do you see?"

Warmth spreads over my cheeks. "Yes," I reply in a soft voice. "Yes, I see very clearly."

MY FONDNESS FOR FRITZ GROWS STRONGER AS THE DAYS pass. Loneliness captures my soul often; the letters I write and receive do not mend my sorrow. Letters from home are generally on the surface and consist of Amy's well-being in Europe. The babies are doubling in size and Teddy excels at school. Beth's spirits remain lifted even though her closest confidant is finding her way in New York.

Fritz distracts me from my grief. There is never a moment where my mind nor my hands are resting. If I am not with the children, I am writing or with Fritz. One evening, I knock on his door with *Hamlet* in hand. We've been lending each other books and it's normal for me to find a novel at my door after a long day.

"Come in!" Inside, Franz and Emil are playing marbles before the heating stove and Fritz sits in a reading chair with a book in hand. "Mees Jo." A smile crosses his face. He removes his spectacles.

"When will you stop calling me Miss Jo?" I ask, finding my way toward the shelves to return the book. His library is my favorite, for none has a librarian as thoughtful as Fritz.

"One day," he confesses, "but not today. How did you like *Hamlet?*"

Franz and Emil are much too preoccupied with their game of marbles to pay attention to me. I walk to Fritz's side and lower onto the arm of the chair.

"It was a mere reread. Nothing new nor exciting. A simple comfort."

"Ah, I understand." He leans an elbow against the opposite arm of the chair.

My gaze falls to the spectacles in his hand. "Can you truly not read without those glasses?"

He gives them to me. "See for yourself."

I flinch when trying them on, the glass blurring my vision and transforming my hand before my face into a brown blob. I slide them off with a laugh to see Fritz's amused face and my heart stills. I don't believe I will ever tire of seeing such admiration in his eyes.

CHAPTER 21

OUR KINGDOM BY THE SEA

At around nine o'clock one evening, I force myself to stop writing because I know I can stay up until dawn without trying.

I wipe my inky hands on my plaid skirt and realize I haven't even changed from my workday clothes. I situate my black vest and re-tuck my blouse before heading downstairs for a glass of water. Even though sensation stories are not my favorite to write, the money helps my family and the stories allow me to experiment with my writing style. I brush off the literary stress of the evening as I pass a closed-off parlor. Muffled voices chat from inside and soon break into laughter.

Most of the scholars who work for Mrs. Kirke are men who have formed an exclusive inner circle. They speak down to each other and have petty drama. With every casual discussion, I find myself in a lecture and learn that they are not much different from a group of schoolgirls. Fritz is often in their presence, but never partakes in their gossip.

As I quench my thirst, the chatter gets louder with the opening of a door. Through the threshold and down the hall-way, I watch men of all shades spill into the foyer. I hear swishing coats through their conversations along with the scuffing of shoes. I set my glass in the sink.

Fritz walks into the kitchen, jumping at my presence. "Mees Jo!" he exclaims, his manner ruffled from a lively gathering.

I offer a polite smile and tuck a loose curl behind my ear. "Professor."

"Oh, call me Fritz, please." His gaze finds my left hand as he fixes his coat collar. "I see you haf been writing tonight."

Heat slides up my neck, for he often asks to see my work. "Oh—yes. It's my first break since dinner."

Fritz's gaze passes between the group of men behind him and me. "Why—you should—why don't you join us? We go to a tavern. It has—uh—the music and dancing and drinks."

My heart clenches; I am barely familiar with the city. Its size daunts me. "Oh—I-I don't know. I shouldn't intrude and I don't know the city and ought I travel with a group of men—I—"

"You will be with me," he says in an amused tone and steps closer. "You trust me, yes? If you are uncomfortable, we leaf. Other women will be there and you do not haf to drink."

My cheeks warm at his eagerness for me to join. I never expect others to rejoice at my company. I tug on the crimson cravat tied loosely around my neck. "Sure," I blurt, reveling in the warmth in my gut at being wanted, "as long as I'm not intruding."

"No, no! Not at all."

"Allow me to gather my shoes and cloak, then."

The men bow their heads with respect when I pass. None of them seems interested in my being there. In fact, I expect them to reject the idea. But once I step into my boots, slide a few coins into my pocket, and secure my ankle-length cloak, the scholars at the bottom of the steps greet me with excitement. Some from drunk joy, some from intrigued joy. I slide my newsboy cap over my head. Fritz offers his arm when we step onto the snowy sidewalk.

I'm not aware of every society rule, but I am sure walking with a group of men down the sidewalk is on the do-not-do list. I have been in this unfamiliar city for over two months; it is time I see more of it.

The streets are rather quiet. Tall oil lamps light the sidewalks coated with snow that crunches beneath my boots. We pass a man smoking a pipe as he leans on a naked tree. The group chatters among themselves and is the loudest on the block. Fritz remains silent as my gaze scours the roads that are usually filled with pedestrians and carriages, but are now bare and scattered with people.

A man with brown skin the same shade as my own is the most curious of the scholars. His name is Professor Mackey and he's a linguist. During the entire journey to the tavern, he tells me about his travels abroad. I slip in a bragging mention of my sister who currently paints her way across Europe. My fingers dig into the rough fabric of Fritz's coat as I fake my interest in Professor Mackey's tales. Once my toes begin growing numb, the group stops before a building and heads inside.

"He always speaks of himself," Fritz whispers.

I chuckle. "You don't say?"

The smell of tobacco fills my nose and chatter bounces from person to person. Not a soul sits alone; everyone is either engaged in discussion or dancing. All shades and genders crowd around us as Fritz guides me through the clouds of smoke. Three musicians on a stage play piano, cello, and an accordion.

We settle at a table on the edge of the dance floor. I must push down the nerves rising in my gut; I don't like to idle by the fire and I crave adventure—and this is it. Fritz takes my cloak and drapes it over a chair he pulls out for me. I remove my newsboy cap, butterflies intensifying at my half-up half-down hairstyle. For a moment, I consider wrapping up my curls in a hasty manner until I drag my gaze over the crowd—women sit on men's laps, women, who wear their hair down, lift their skirts above their knees as they fan their dancing sweat away, and some men are dressed in women's clothes! This place is liberated, free, and exactly what I want. I shake my hair and pull it over my shoulder.

"Would you like a drink?" Fritz asks. Professor Mackey lowers at the table and hands a tin cup to Fritz.

I inhale as my butterflies of anxiety turn to eagerness. "I would, but I'm not sure what to get!"

"Well"—he clears his throat and points to his drink—"*this* is beer, but—"

"May I?" I ask and gesture toward the cup. At his acceptance, I sip beer for the first time. The sour, rotten taste spreads over my tongue and poisons my mouth. It's such a horrid taste I cannot keep a respectable, passive expression. Fritz and the others laugh.

"Wine, then!" he exclaims, to which I nod.

The time that follows holds a place in my heart for eternity. My leniency with my behavior in society pales in comparison to this seemingly rule-free establishment. Here, I'm confronted with my small-town upbringing as I dance and twirl with various partners to never-ending melodies from the musicians on stage. Those I dance with don't concern themselves with making matches or appearing how society deems appropriate. This is not the place I would imagine Mrs. Kirke's scholars to enjoy, but the moment I see Professor Mackey engaged in a kiss with another man, realization sprinkles over me. Eyes holding no judgment reside here.

After twenty minutes of dancing, I stumble over to the table, out of breath with my heart racing, and into a literary conversation. I snatch a random pamphlet on the table and fan myself. I don't hike my skirt over my knees, but I certainly empathize with the people who do.

"No respectable writer uses such topics," says Fritz, leaning on the table with his shirtsleeves rolled up to his elbows.

"Truth!" says one of the scholars—Professor Johnson.

"The man's interests are different than yours," Professor Mackey argues. "No need to crucify him for that."

Fritz shakes his head as he absentmindedly hands me my cup of wine. "It is not a matter of difference. It's—"

Professor Mackey gestures toward me. "Wait—why don't you ask the lady her thoughts on it? A female opinion may give you more perspective."

My thundering heart begins to settle. I sip wine and run my hand over my head to smooth back curls that broke free from my ribbon. "My opinion stands on its own, but I shall gladly grant my perspective on the topic!"

"All right, then"—Fritz settles his arm over the back of his chair to turn toward me—"uh—Edgar Allan Poe. Your thoughts on him."

"Excellent writer! He has created a new genre!"

Snickers erupt around the table. Professor Mackey drums his hands on the wooden surface and exclaims, "There you have it!"

"No, no," says Professor Johnson.

"I am surprised, Jo!" Fritz tells me, tugging on his beard.

I am often crucified for my opinion; I would much rather be in a debate about literature than about a woman's role or respectability. "Why is that? Oh! Allow me to guess; you believed me to adore the swooning love poems of Wordsworth and Blake?"

"Not at all! These gentleman certainly haf, but I imagine you a fan of Coleridge or Tennyson."

"Mm!" I hum as I rush to gulp my mouthful of wine.

"Indeed, you are correct!" My gaze falls aside as I dredge up an old memorization of Coleridge. "*The wrinkled sea beneath him crawls / He watches from his mountain walls—*"

"*And like a thunderbolt he falls,*" Fritz completes. Admiration glimmers in his eyes.

I smile. "I may adore more than one genre."

"But Poe—his work is—morbid, inappropriate, and immoral."

"Do you believe *me* immoral for reading and liking his work?"

"I—"

"You are blinded by general view of him without developing your own opinion. You may find his works indeed with meaning, *buried* under the morbid tones. Have you ever considered he does that purposefully?"

"Ends do not always justify the means, Miss March," Professor Johnson says, and it's one of the few times he's addressed me directly.

I confess that part of my defensiveness is rooted in my secret writing gig with *The Weekly Volcano*. Fantastical stories may very well include moral tones, but I begin to understand Dashwood's reasoning for publishing stories solely for enjoyment. The world has enough evil—sometimes we want to feel good for but a short period of time. I wave a dismissive hand and throw my elbow over the back of the chair. "Writers are meant to bend the rules."

"Writers haf no obligation to anybody but themselves and *moral* writers keep in mind that the children and youth who read their work are easily influenced," Fritz says in a firm voice.

"I agree with you, Miss March. Writers are the leading forces of following generations and they should be encouraged, not knocked down."

In a spell of passion (and wine), my chair scrapes as I slide back and rise, gripping Fritz's elbow to rise with me. I use his shoulder for support while I step onto the seat. The staring and the constant bustling and shoving of patrons make me shrink into myself. I push aside insecurity, clear my throat, and bellow Poe's poem in an effort to prove his work is not as immoral and poisonous as Fritz and others act. With a hand on Fritz's shoulder to keep me upright, I chant to the unruly crowd:

> "It was many and many a year ago,
> In a kingdom by the sea,
> That a maiden there lived whom you
>   may know
> By the name of Annabel Lee;
> And this maiden she lived with no other
>   thought
> Than to love and be loved by me.
> *I* was a child and *she* was a child,
> In this kingdom by the sea
> But we—"

A stumbling patron knocks into me, and my impaired state takes my balance and throws me from the chair. I fall into Fritz, who wraps his arms around me and turns us away so I can find my footing. Yet all I find are my arms looping his neck, our faces inches apart, and my feet hardly keeping me upright.

"But, uh, we what?" he asks.

His embrace sends nerves dancing up my core and wrapping around my heart. I inhale, fighting to catch my breath and keep focus, but his eyes capture mine hostage. "We loved with a — with a love that was... more than love"

He clears his throat. "Perhaps I ought to—to read his work... before I make judgment."

I slowly stand up straight, adoring every precarious moment

in his proximity. The corner of my lips lifts as I slide my hands down his arms. "Perhaps." I wrap my hands around his. "Dance with me."

Fritz blinks and gathers himself. "I'm sorry?"

"Dance with me," I repeat, backing toward the dance floor and pulling him with me. *"Tanz mit mir."*

He startles at my sudden German; a smile breaks free while he lifts one arm and tugs me closer with the other. "You haf been practicing."

"Ein bisschen. Can you teach me more?"

As we step into the dance, he says earnestly, "I would be honored."

CHAPTER 22

LOSING WITS

The night at the tavern inspires me to continue educating myself.

It was refreshing to not sit on the outskirts of a conversation. The men, albeit not void of their condescending natures, listen to and value my opinion.

Night falls upon New York City. The children either sleep or occupy themselves with games in other rooms. Six men and I sit in the parlor—Fritz and Professor Mackey included. They're speaking of religion, a topic I am not educated in but also not a stranger to. I sit beside Fritz on the couch.

"If there's a God, where is he when all of these people are starving without a penny to their name?" asks one of the men with a pipe in hand. His name is Professor Boyd.

Fritz bristles in his seat and scratches his beard. "Gott doesn't gif you anything you can't handle."

I find myself agreeing more with Professor Boyd, who stands by the fireplace with an elbow on the mantel. I square my shoulders and ask Fritz with genuine curiosity, "Where is the proof of that?"

My voice startles the room because I've been silent most of

the conversation. He turns to me and says in a simple tone, "The Bible, Mees Marsch."

I don't miss the way he adopts formality in front of the men. Ever since the night at the tavern, he reserves informalities for when we are alone. When we are around others, he remains distant.

"The Bible has gone through many translations," I say. "How can we trust it was written by God?"

"It wasn't written by Gott. It was written by Jesus."

My breath catches as the sense of inadequacy hovers over me. I ignore it. "Right, but how can we trust Jesus?"

"Exactly, Miss March, thank you," Professor Boyd says, which sends a surge of confidence through me. He turns to the other men. "The lady is right."

"How can you ask such a thing?" Fritz asks with an incredulous expression. "A man with so much influence has no other explanation than to be touched by Gott Himself. He was birthed by Virgin Mary and by Gott—he was their child."

"How—"

"Gott is the creation of everything." His voice raises and his cheeks adopt a tinge of red. "There is no denying that, and it would do you well to learn it. John 8:32 explains that Jesus has knowledge of the world before his birth. In Isaiah 40:3, there are witnesses to proof that Gott is his father. And in Matthew 3:16, Gott Himself claims Jesus as his offspring."

It isn't that I don't believe in God—because I do. I pray to Him and I serve Him, but I disagree with the people who use Him to excuse the monstrosities of the world. Too many hide behind a faulty book and take it as their reason for hatred. A couple of men make sounds as they begin to protest, but my voice cuts them off, for Fritz's condescending demeanor lifts my temper. He has never acted this way toward me.

"The only evidence to support that is a book that has gone

through many translations and could have very well been written by a man who lost his wits."

Anger flashes over his face and he shifts toward me. "A man who lost his wits could not have influenced that many people."

"I disagree. Many people in society believe a woman's place is beneath men, but all of them have certainly lost their wits to believe such a thing."

"Are you saying I'm a man who's lost my wits?"

"Are you saying you believe women to be beneath you?" I reply before my mind has a chance to consider.

Fritz snickers. He rubs his hand over his face and tugs his beard as he searches for words. "I find it ironic that a girl whose father is a minister to say such ghastly things against the words of Christ. I should think he raised you better."

I've remained calm through the discussion, but it is clear he takes my stance personally and decides to undermine my intelligence. I rally my temper the best I can, but I cannot promise myself it won't fly.

"I beg your pardon?"

"You are only a child—"

"And you are only a pompous, arrogant man who cannot stand to admit when he's been bested—least of all by a woman." Well, too late to control my temper. With the men's eyes on us, I rise to my feet and dust off my skirt. "I suggest you mend that fatal flaw before you find yourself friendless and alone, professor. I bid you goodnight."

Every day, Fritz regards me as an equal. I never had to earn his respect the way I had with the other scholars. It seems his high regard is not as genuine as I once thought. The possibility sends an ache shuddering through my body, especially through my heart.

Aside from Teddy, Fritz is the first man I've grown close to. Except he's incomparable to Teddy, for they're much too different. My time with the professor has helped me grow into the person I want to be. Over these months, I believed our friendship much too sacred to lose over a small argument.

It takes me hours to fall asleep that night. I distract my mind by concocting more tales to add to my list of ideas. By the following morning, I'm cross and tired. I smother a yawn as I gather contents for tea because Lucy and Agnes like to enjoy a cup each morning before lessons.

Behind me, a deep voice clears his throat. "Goot morning," Fritz says, then adds, "I was out of line last night—"

"Yes, you were," I interject, my back still to him.

He sighs. "It is that—I am very passionate about my religion."

I face him with the assumption that my anger may have subsided overnight, but agitation flares at his weak excuse. "There is a difference between passion, and flying at anyone who disagrees with you. One is admirable, the other is self-righteous."

"Mees Marsch, I am trying to apologize."

"I'm still Miss March, am I?" I ask, loathing the mournful pang shuddering through my gut. "An apology is but a sentence. You insulted my father and questioned my intelligence. You may say sorry and then return to the same defense when the conversation arises once more. I have respect for everyone's religious beliefs. And you believed incorrectly last night, for I *do* believe in God, merely in a different way than you. I should like to reserve the right for you to respect my belief as I do yours." I turn and snatch the tray before shouldering past him. "If you'll excuse me, *Professor Bhaer*, I have children to teach."

OUR ENCOUNTERS ARE AWKWARD OVER THE NEXT FEW weeks. Conversations are mere exchanges regarding the children. When arriving home from meeting with Mr. Dashwood one afternoon, I find a bundle of flowers and a book in front of my bedroom door. My cheeks warm—not from the flowers, but from the blatant display of remorse. Fritz is private and always slow to admit when he's wrong. To apologize in an apparent manner, where nosy children pass through the hallways, brings me gratitude and turns my cheeks red. It tells me how much I mean to him.

A beloved memory resurfaces from years ago when Teddy invited Meg and me to the theater because he knew I would like it. To be thought of as an individual, to have another go out of their way for your benefit, may seem unremarkable and natural. But sometimes it impacts you more than expected, makes you feel noticed more than usual, and adored by simply being who you are.

After I take the book and flowers into my bedroom, a knock echoes at the door. I believe it to be Fritz until Mrs. K's gentle smile greets me.

"Here you go, dear," she says, handing me an envelope. My heart tightens when I realize it's from home. I haven't yet responded to my family's last letter. I tear it open once I close the door behind her.

DEAREST JO,

DO NOT FRET—THE FAMILY IS SAFE AND IN GOOD SPIRITS. I WON'T MAKE THIS LETTER LONG AND WILL HASTEN MY INTENTION. I MISS YOU DEARLY. I HATE TO BURDEN YOUR RESPONSIBILITIES IN NEW YORK. I'VE HELD STEADY FOR MONTHS, BUT I CAN NO LONGER. PLEASE COME HOME, JO.

EVER YOURS,

BETH

My hands tremble. *I've held steady for months, but I can no longer.* The darkness hovering around my heart says she withheld something. Terror seizes my being in an unexplainable grip.

"Jo?"

The voice startles me and I press a palm against my chest. Fritz rests a hand on my shoulder and warily approaches. I hand him the letter and begin pacing. Whatever troubles Beth deeper than what she wrote, the fault is mine. I left. I abandoned her for my selfish wishes. Part of me knows the reason behind Beth's troubles. I fear admitting it will make it true. She hasn't been the same since having scarlet fever. Her energy and strength dwindle with each season.

"She misses you," Fritz says in a gentle voice. "Why are you—"

"Something else troubles her deeply. I know it. I know my sister." My voice cracks on the final word. Fritz stops my pacing by taking both of my shoulders. He catches my eyes.

"Then you go home. Do not worry about what you don't know." After a moment of my hesitation, he adds, "Okay?"

I inhale and nod. "Okay." I place my hand over his and toss a glance at my strewn clothes over the floor. There is packing to be done, but I am sure my mind will wander to Beth. I hold Fritz's hand tighter and press my cheek to his fingers. "Please... talk to me."

"What about?"

"Anything. Talk to me, please."

He carefully regards me. "Of course."

Mrs. K understands as soon as I tell her. If anything, the dreadful look on my face convinced her. Because my train leaves at sunrise, all goodbyes occur the night prior. The children are next to inconsolable when learning of my early departure. It saddens me to leave them, but Beth means much more.

Fritz notices my distress and promises to accompany me for my early departure.

When I venture to my bedroom for sleep I know I won't find, he tracks me down in the hallway. I haven't had the chance to tell him that I forgive him; my worried soul is much too preoccupied to give it much thought now. I turn to him, grateful for the distraction; my room holds nothing but anxious thoughts waiting for me.

"What is it?"

"I only want to say—" Fritz breaks off, slicking a hand through his hair before tugging his beard. He squares his shoulders. "I-I admire you, Mees Marsch—Jo. You are strong and willful and I very much like spending time with you. You teach me a great deal. I haf not realized how much I need to learn until I met you."

It almost sounds like a declaration of affection. "Professor B—"

"Fritz," he insists, stepping closer and wringing his hands together. "To you, I haf *always* been Fritz."

The ache in his eyes reaches into my heart and twists. I cannot give myself to him. Not now, not soon. I must save my strength and love for Beth. "I... I'm leaving tomorrow."

"I know, and I wish not to keep you from your family"—he bows his head and steps back—"nor this boy you seem to admire."

"Who?" I tilt my head. "Teddy? No, I admire Teddy as my best friend." I reach for his hand. "That is all he is to me."

"Oh. *Gut,* then." Relief flutters over his face. "As you said, you leaf tomorrow. I will say no more; I don't wish to make your departure difficult."

My cheeks warm and I let sentiment rise for but a moment. I squeeze his hand. "Leaving you will never be easy."

THE FOLLOWING MORNING, AFTER AN HOUR OF SLEEP, Fritz brings me to the train station. I wear a brown skirt with a white blouse and my usual black vest. My hair twists into a loose bun at my nape. I complete the outfit with a big sun hat in case I want to rest my eyes during the journey. I set down my suitcase for a proper goodbye.

Fritz takes my hand and squeezes. "I am sure she is okay."

I nod despite knowing he says this for my benefit. "You must visit," I insist, taking his other hand and stepping in front of him. "I shall never forgive you if you don't."

I cannot decipher whether his red cheeks are from blushing or the morning chill. Summer approaches, but chilly remnants scatter through the air.

"I shall."

"Next month. Teddy graduates then and you'd enjoy the commencement." His face dims, but I hold fast and shift closer. I fear he still believes I care for Teddy more than a dear friend. "Oh, do say yes, Fritz. I should truly wish for everyone to meet the man I've written to them about so often."

His expression relaxes, replaced by the usual face of adoration. "Yes, of course. I promise." He inhales. "I will miss you very much."

I open my mouth to respond, but a conductor shouts—much too loudly for an early train—for all to board. "That's me," I mutter, dropping one of his hands to pick up my suitcase. I walk toward the train without releasing his other hand. Our arms stretch between us.

"Goodbye, Jo."

"Goodbye, Fritz."

I let his hand fall and secure my hat. The conductor volunteers to take my bag, which I allow. I look back to Fritz, who watches me with longing. His brown hair has a slight curl to it, with a strand falling beautifully onto his forehead as his kind eyes convey the frown his beard smothers.

Much has changed over the past few years. Meg married with children. Amy off to Europe. Teddy in college. Everyone follows their dreams and I've been doing the same, traveling and writing. Along the way, I met Fritz. He somehow became a healthy piece of my heart. I'm still unsure of what is considered romantic, for I feel no connection to such emotions, but I know my life is richer with him in it. And I should want him to know that.

The conductor waits for me to find my seat, but I hop off the train and dart toward Fritz. My hat flies off. Confusion crosses the professor's face. I ignore it; I take his bearded cheeks in my hands and press my lips to his. It stuns him at first but doesn't take long for him to sink into my kiss and rest his hands on my back. If it were midday and crowded, I would scandalize us. But scandalization is what I'm known for, so I savor the coffee taste of his mouth and wrap my arms around his neck. My stomach flutters with desire as his lips slide over mine.

"I'll miss you too," I whisper, pressing my forehead to his.

Fritz smiles and brushes a curl from my face, his thumb grazing my cheek. "I will see you soon, my dear."

Chapter 23

Arrivals and Departures

My heart still possesses tenderness from leaving Fritz, but the joy upon my homecoming proves the most efficient healing tonic. Mother, Father, Hannah, and Meg's surprised reactions are enough to send me into good spirits. I spend a few extra moments in Beth's embrace, whispering that all is well now that I'm home.

When Teddy comes over, I am sure his feelings for me have died until his kiss presses against my head. It may very well mean nothing, for we've done such kisses many times before, but my anxious mind takes over my logic. The joy of my arrival lasts all evening, and I fall asleep before asking Beth about her troubles.

I find Beth gone by the time I wake. Marmee says she spends most of her time at Meg's, which comforts me. It means that my sister hasn't spent time with only Mother and Father; she leaves the house and walks every day.

Apprehension hovers my shoulders when Teddy asks if I wish to go rowing on the river with him. I accept the invitation despite knowing in my heart that something would happen. We pass down the hillside toward the canoe.

"You're a graduate now!" I say, picking up the oar. "What will you do now? Sail away?"

"I have something in mind." He stops walking and slides his hands into his pockets. His tender gaze falls upon me and I know that the dreadful moment has come.

My chest tightens and I drop the oar and start up the hill as if I can run away from this, but he trails behind me. "No, Teddy. Don't—please."

"Jo, we've got to have it out," he insists. "You must hear me at last!"

For years, our relationship has teetered. It has remained the same in my heart; I fear he doesn't understand that. Perhaps he's right and we must have it out at last. This way, he can move on and our friendship will be fresh and beautiful again. I stop walking and turn toward him, wiping my sweaty palms on my skirt.

"All right. I'll listen."

Teddy sighs and speaks in a resolute tone. "I've loved you ever since I've known you, Jo. I couldn't help it. You wouldn't let me show it, but I must have an answer because I can't go on like this."

The soft expression his face holds sends a wave of hurt through me. I hate to cause him pain. I press a hand against my stomach. "I wanted to save you this. I..."

"I know, but girls are odd and you never know what they mean. No means yes and—"

"*No.* I have always meant what I said."

"Your actions don't meet your words! You kiss me but tell me to forget everything, and I did—for Beth and your father. And then the wedding—" He huffs. "I've tried so hard to be who you want me to be." His shoulders fall. "I know I'm not half as good enough—"

"No, no!" I protest. "You are amazing. You're a great deal

too good for me and I'm so grateful for you and proud of you." I release him. My words are knives in my throat. "I don't know why I can't love you as I should, dear. But I don't."

Teddy flinches, falling back a step and studying me with a surprised look. "Really, truly?"

"Really, truly." For a moment, I believe the hard part is over. But his despondent expression worsens as he walks away. I cannot let my friend leave in such a tender-hearted state. "I'm so sorry. I'm so desperately sorry. I wish I could. What about those lovely girls you wrote about? Have any of those flames—"

He whirls toward me with sudden anger. "Oh, stop it, Jo. I told you about them to try and get a rise out of you, but you did nothing. Every time, it was like you had no heart for me. Those girls meant nothing!" He wipes his fingers over his mouth as if his words are poison. "Each time I came back from school, you felt like home again! Not that mansion, not Grandfather, not Brooke—*you!*"

I hold my hands against my chest, for I can feel my own heart breaking as I'm wounding someone I'd fight wars for. Tears threaten to rise. "Teddy, you have to know that I've tried to love you in that way. I tried everything I could but I—*I can't!*"

"Then why have you kissed me?" he asks fiercely.

"I was trying to convince myself to love you and I failed. We are much too stubborn and our wills are much too strong to *ever* make a happy match."

Teddy grips my elbow with desperation, his eyes boring into mine. "I would be a perfect saint to you, Jo March. You could turn me into anything you—"

My voice cracks. "No! That isn't what love should be. You are not mine to toy with! You're a person of your own and—"

"Where is this coming from?"

"I have always felt this way."

"No, you haven't."

"I have."

"No! You—"

"Be reasonable, my boy."

"No, I won't! I won't be reasonable!" he shouts, grabbing his heart. "Don't you understand what you do to me? You have a hook inside my heart and you're shredding me to pieces!"

A tear escapes and I wipe it away before it reaches my cheek. He gives me such power and influence I never asked for nor wanted. I never want control over a person, least of all someone I care about this much. "I am not worthy of such an obligation. Please don't do that to me."

"Tell me what it is I need to do to make you love me."

"There is nothing. And I should tell you something."

He scowls and walks up the hill. If not for the dreadful conversation, the day is beautiful—with clear skies and a refreshing breeze. "Oh, don't! Don't tell me this."

I follow with confusion. "Tell you what?"

"That you're in love with that old man."

"Old man? What are you—"

"That devilish professor you always wrote about! Don't you tell me you love him because he can do *nothing* for you and—"

I push his shoulder with a wave of irritation flooding me. "Don't speak ill of my dear professor! He isn't old nor anything bad. He is good and kind and very important to me. I know I shall get cross and angry if you abuse him! I have no intention of marrying—"

"Lies. You love him."

"Stop it. I am happy as I am and I'm trying to say that I don't—"

Teddy cuts me off by taking my waist and pulling me to him. Unlike the other times, I shove him away before anything happens.

"I said stop it!" I yell. "I've done my best to be reasonable because I don't want to hurt you. But I will *never* marry you, Theodore Laurence. You are my best friend and I care about you so much. *We have tried our way and it doesn't work!* You have shown me much about what I want and what I don't. And I have showed you what love *shouldn't* do to a person and one day you'll see and thank me for it. I shouldn't stir you like this, Teddy. That is not love."

For a time, I found myself wrapped in the tug-and-pull of us; it was exciting and new, and I understood we have a special bond, quite unlike other friendships. I confess I hadn't wanted our game to end for a long while. Teddy made me feel like walking on the edge of a cliff, showing me how much power I can hold. It was fun to love and be loved and experiment with how much I want from a life partner. But we have grown into adults and it's time to acknowledge that we make a horrible match. He continues to live in the mindset we had at ages fifteen and sixteen and we may very well live as those children— as friends. It is the only way for us to continue in one another's lives, for anything else would cause a catastrophe and my dear boy is smart enough to know that; he needs time to see this.

"I love you, Jo," he says at last.

I try to adopt a gentle voice to soften the blunt nature of my words. "For now. You will get over it, my boy, now that we've had it out."

THE EVENING CONSISTS OF TIME AT DOVECOTE. I TRY TO focus on the babies rather than the occurrence of the afternoon. As I spend time with Daisy and Demi, Meg and John clean and dry dishes. Beth sits at the kitchen table, dividing flowers and herbs she picked today. Meg and Beth must be spending more time in the garden; their complexions are browner than usual.

Daisy runs up to Meg to show her the new toy I brought. My sister, weary and tired, welcomes her with feigned enthusiasm. Exhaustion falls upon the two little parents most endearingly. It excites me to see Meg with such diligent responsibilities. She pours her life into these tiny babies and seeing her with them sends a pang of jealousy through my body. The feeling approaches before I can prepare myself, for I've never had such an interest in motherhood before. More so, I have not considered it—and I had put off the thoughts at the sight of Marmee so overworked from her children.

After adoring my work with Agnes and Lucy over the winter and spring, I discovered a yearning to nurture and guide children, though, admittedly, my penchant for bossing others around is partly to blame. My heart expands knowing I may act as the beacon of knowledge for their curious minds. However, the influence a mother figure holds can change generations. And, from the way Daisy looks at Meg with a child's genuine love, I crave being cared about in such a way.

"Laurie proposed to me," I blurt from my spot on the ground.

Meg whirls around, a pot in hand with her jaw slack. John's gaze snaps to me and Beth halts her dividing.

"I guess congratulations are in order," John says.

Meg sets the pot on the counter. "John, leave."

"What?" He blinks, exchanging confused looks between Meg and me.

"Oh, no," Beth whispers as she realizes that congratulations are *not* in order, and I won't be making Teddy a brother-in-law. It dawns on me that my older sister is the only one who knows I never cared for him in that way. I rise and slide into a seat.

"Oh," John gasps. "I'll leave you girls to it, then."

Meg slides into the chair across from me. "Please do. The

babies are fine here if you like." She reaches over and takes my hands. "How did he take it?"

"I don't understand," Beth admits. "I thought you loved him."

"Not in a romantic manner. Never in that way." I sigh. "I fear our friendship will never be the same. Oh, Meg, it was dreadful! You should have seen the look on his face. It is as if I tore his whole life apart!"

"I'm so sorry, dear. I'm sure he will come to his senses."

"I truly believed you loved him, Jo."

Beth's words send a painful ache through my heart, though I'm sure she means no harm. I failed one of the utmost important tasks, the most important expectation. Why, how cruel I must be! I cannot complete a simple wish that would make everyone content—everyone but myself.

"I... I'm sorry."

"Sorry?" Meg echoes as she pries away Demi from trying to climb the cupboard. "Whatever for?"

"Why?"

The request to explain my failure only makes it harder. Tears try to fill my eyes; I shove them down. "I tried—I really tried. All I've ever wanted to do is make this family proud. And I—I keep failing. I keep ruining it all."

I should have been here sooner for Beth. I should be able to love Laurie. I never should have written those stories...

"You've accomplished so much," Meg say, wrapping her arms around me. "You should be proud."

Beth rises to join the hug. "You haven't failed at all."

I don't reply; I clench my jaw. Speaking of any kind will break the dam and my tears will be unstoppable. I sit in my sisters' embrace and let them bring my spirit home.

CHAPTER 24

A ROOM FOR YOU

Finally, I insist on Beth and I taking a trip. She believes the mountains to be too far from home, so we settle for a beach trip. I've written to Fritz with a profuse apology—that it isn't a good time for him to visit.

After I rejected Teddy, he fled to Europe. It sets me at ease; it will help him heal and he will be with Amy, who I suspect has been homesick.

Beth and I spend our days inside an endearing beach house. We savor the blinding sun resting against the white sand and soft waves. Mornings and nights, we walk along the shore. It doesn't ever last very long—Beth tires easily these days. One of them, she'll tell me the reason.

I gasp, leaning down and snatching a seashell with swirling blue-and-white hues. "Look at this one!"

Beth leans over my shoulder. "It's beautiful."

The breeze whips my hair across my face. I brush it off and hold the shell to her eyes. "You match."

She grins, her freckled cheeks curving. She takes the shell and places it in her tiny basket. "Imagine if all of these shells were a dozen little eyes—watching over you."

"In a protective or odd manner?" I ask, half distracted by the brown shell in my hand. I toss it into the water.

"Protective, of course."

I wrap my arms around her and peck her cheek. "Then I'm your seashell."

"You're my seashell."

"Protective and watching over you. I take my job very seriously."

Beth chuckles. "Look—those girls again! Are you sure you don't want to join their picnic? They seemed agreeable."

We pass the same girls on our walks each day. Yesterday, we stopped and talked for a moment. They seem agreeable enough but I am not on this trip to make friends. I'm here to be with Beth.

"We have a picnic of our own," I remind her, taking her hand and guiding us up the beach. We leave tomorrow, and she still hasn't told me about her troubles. Thus, when we finish eating and I plop my head in her lap, I blurt, "Out with it, dear. All of it. I must learn the reason behind your pain."

My words don't surprise her. Her gaze lingers on the ocean, her lips shaking as if she's fighting for control over the ability to speak. "I... I've been mourning for months now."

"Mourning?" I ask, trying to remember whose funeral I forgot about. "Who—Pip? It wasn't—"

"No, Jo. I've been mourning myself."

My stomach tightens. I rise and watch her with a struck expression. Like her, my lips fight for control. "I... I don't..."

"It's okay." Beth gives me a reassuring smile, but the sadness behind her eyes tells me she doesn't believe it. "I had a small ceremony for myself and it was... it was more comforting than I imagined."

My breath catches. *Mourning. Ceremonies.* "Oh... no. No, Beth. *No.*"

I suspected as such; I refused to let myself go there. Nothing ever goes my way, so if I *had* considered it, she would be getting healthier instead of getting sicker.

"I've tried to fight it, dear. But I can't." After moments of my silence, she turns toward the water. "I somehow knew. You all… you're all beautiful little floods on the shores. I've always been a mere wave."

"You are everything to us," I insist, gripping her hand and letting my words inform her as well as myself. "We can't get on without you."

"Don't make me feel guilty for something I can't control," she snaps in a broken voice. I fall silent; she's never snapped at me before. "I don't want to die. I've tried with all my might, but I don't believe my spirit has ever been long for this world."

My eyes burn with tears. I hate admitting I've thought the same. When picturing my future, Beth's spot has always been blurry. I lower my gaze, clenching my jaw and tugging at loose threads on the blanket to distract me. "God can't take you from us. I'll… I'll stand up to Him."

"I know you will," she says, then adds, "I'm not afraid."

"I am," I scoff, and continue battling the flood of tears. The seagulls continue cawing and squawking. *Do they ever stop?*

"I used to be. But I've prepared myself."

Her lingering tone and the troubling nature of her face make me hesitate. "What is it?" I press.

"There's someone waiting for me."

I don't understand at first. When I settle on a guess, I'm not sure how I came to it. It's an old, distant memory that I thought I'd forgotten about. The girl and the cottage. The girl Beth called—

"Lucy."

She lowers her head. "Yes. I'm in no rush. I don't want to go. But I'll be with her."

"In your little cottage," I say, detesting the idea of someone else living with my sister. She belongs with the family.

"Ever since the fever, I see her in dreams—when I sleep so deeply that I wake with a gasp... But I feel safe every time I see her," she says in a meek voice. "She loves me very much."

The certainty in her voice comforts me. It makes me believe Lucy is real and she will surely be living with someone who will love and care for her. I know now why she hesitates, for it's not often where we see a girl loving another girl.

Beth lifts her head toward me. "Do you find it strange?"

"From someone incapable of sentimental love, any love at all is of the utmost beauty." I place my hand over hers, my throat thickening with emotion. "I will miss you very much."

She purses her lips and nods. "We will have a room made up for you."

I chuckle through my incoming tears. "Be sure it has an inkstand."

"Of course."

"And books."

"Always. Promise me one thing, Jo, dear."

"Anything you wish."

"Be in no hurry to join me in the cottage. Time will carry you to me eventually. Live as long as you can, so you can tell me stories. Please—I want to know all of the stories."

Her words make tears flow harder, for she understands me so very well. My next thought was when I met with her again. When I could meet Lucy and live with her in the little cottage. I manage a weak promise and we try to savor the last drops of our trip to the beach.

She soon wanders among the shore. Her attention snaps to me when a little gull perches on her hand. We both grin and smother our laughs. Such a rarity a bird visits this close to humans!

The image of Beth creates a hole in my mind and heart. Sunlight shimmers against the white sand she stands upon. The waves flow behind her in beautiful strides upon the shore, its foam bubbling almost in the shape of a dozen hearts just for her. The white-winged little peep sits on her hand in a content manner, fluffing its feathers as she smiles. Beth's curls shake behind her in the breeze and her skirt ruffles against her legs. If I were Amy, I would paint the scene. Perhaps if I describe it to the little artist...

My heart shines when Beth's smile turns to me. Happiness radiates from her rosy cheeks and I pray to God that He keeps them rosy. But I know He won't. I enjoy Beth's joy and dread the day I will ever lose her.

Marmee and Papa need no words upon our arrival. It pleases me in a twisted way; it spares me from telling my parents their worst nightmare is bound to come true. The most comfortable room is set aside for Beth—the study. We transport a bed and a chaise and fill it with flowers, pictures, her little piano, and her cats. Meg brings the babies often to lift Beth's spirits. We ensure the room is filled with all she pleases. Little school children pass the house every day, even when school is not in session. They pop their sweet faces in the window and smile.

For a time, while in bed, Beth remains the busiest she's ever been. She knits for them—mittens, scarves, and even a sweater. A guest stops by her window every hour of the day until the sun goes down. Gifts and prayers never leave our doorstep, for mournful souls rumble endlessly through Concord. Who would have guessed! The quietest, most serene little girl pulls the entire town together in a few short weeks.

Meg has been creating costumes and dresses for the local theater and enlists Beth's help, for our ill sister is always eager to be of use. My lack of adequate sewing skills results in my being the mannequin for them to test the results on. We sit in the study—Beth's room—with the family gathered and the babies crawling or walking with wobbling legs.

"Careful—!" Meg exclaims, reaching out a hand toward Demi.

"Let him wander, dear," John says, a hand on her back. "He must learn to get up when he falls."

I dearly wish Amy were here. Meg has John and the babies and Mother has Father as we all prepare for Beth's permanent departure.

I write to Fritz when I can. He understands why it is a bad idea for him to visit. I didn't tell him about Laurie's proposal in case he thinks I considered saying yes. Nonetheless, I am much too busy with Beth to handle such drama. It infuriates me that, knowing of my sister's condition, Laurie continued to send me a letter in hope that I reconsider his proposal. Even now, as I sit with my family, the anger sneaks up again. All I wish for is Beth's health. It is the one desire on my mind and my one duty. I never leave her side for more than an hour.

Marmee sits beside me on the chaise. She's the only person who knows of the second proposal. She speaks in a low voice. "Are you still upset over Laurie?"

"Of course I am." I look down, lest my irritated expression worries Beth. "How could he do that?"

"He has not come to his senses yet. That's all, dear. His heart is tender. Be gentle with your reply."

I try to heed my wise mother's advice and rein my temper. One afternoon, Beth requests my departure, which troubles me greatly. She bids John to join her in the study and wants no one to enter. After an hour, John beckons Marmee. More silence.

Later, they flee the study without so much of an inkling about what they spoke of. I don't ask Beth about it, for I'm sure she will tell me if I should know.

Beth falls quieter as the days pass. She observes often and smiles constantly. One night, I find her staring at the wall, her gaze unfocused but her lips and brows quirked in a tranquil sort of way. If not for her blinking and moving chest, I would have feared the worst. When I find her that way again the next afternoon, I decipher that she slips more from the world of the living as she prepares herself for the dead.

It is a peaceful yet painful process—Beth's death. At once, she is granted the chance to prepare herself. She may set her affairs in order and let her soul transition. I sob at the thought of having no new memories with her. But the wait is excruciating. Every morning, I wake with the fear there is one less soul in this house. With each nap of Beth's, I watch over her, frightened that her chest will stop rising and falling. I wonder often *"is this the day?"* and loathe myself for wanting the darkness to finally arrive, for I am desperate to alleviate this agonizing wait.

One morning, I walk into the study with Beth's milk. She sits in her bed, twirling a sunflower between her fingers. When I set the tray on her bedside table, I notice the tremble of her body and hear a sniffle.

"What is it?" I lower onto the edge. "Are you in pain?"

What I believe to be a sob at first turns out to be a laugh. She looks up and meets me with a genuine grin. Joy fills her face and tears flow from her eyes. I, too, find myself smiling. I wipe away one of her tears.

"Why are you crying?"

Beth holds the sunflower to her chest. "I'm—I'm the luckiest girl in the world."

I smother my flinch. She prepares for death at the young age of nineteen—and declares herself lucky. Now, I'm afraid she's lost her wits and will begin calling me Marmee again.

"Beth—"

"I have a home. A house. The most loving family a girl can have," she explains, watching me with a gentle expression. "It may have been uneventful, as I've had no ambitions other than joy, but I've had exactly what I wanted. Joy. I blossom in rosy sunsets and hold peace when with my cats. And I've always been full of the love my family has for me. Especially the love from my seashell." She takes my hand and now it's my turn for a smile. A few of my tears escape me for a reason I cannot fathom. My forehead touches hers.

"I have softened my heart for death," Beth continues. "My tender sorrow will never die, but I pray it blooms as your favorite flower."

"That sounds like a poem."

"Write it for me, then."

"I shall." I lift my head and tuck a strand of hair behind her ear. "And I shall call it 'My Seashell, My Flower, My Beth.'"

"Write it for me when I'm gone."

My sadness strengthens and my face dims. "I..."

Beth kisses my cheek. "I know exactly how much I mean to you. Write the poem. Write it again. Bury one of them in the garden and it will blossom in mine."

CHAPTER 25

MY SEASHELL, MY FLOWER, MY BETH

Flower waits for the sun with content
  petals,
tuneful rhythms flowing from her heart
  and into grateful souls.
The sisterly flower I hold dear,
oh—do pass in tranquility!
You leave the world without fear.
Bequeath me your mystified joy before
  sinking into rivers.
No seashell shall ever be normal!
A dozen little eyes resting upon the sand
  which
curve around willing toes inching
  toward
rest without pain.
I carry thy hand upon departure.
My Beth, I beg thy cottage to protect
  thee.
My flower, the tenderest sorrow burdens

my bosom without death, but she indeed
    blooms.
My seashell, you become my guardian,
your watchful eyes holding me with
    gentle palms,
leaving behind a well-behaved girl who
    vies for your pride.
My dearest, you've blossomed in tragic
    simplicity.
You hold a grateful town hostage in your
    heart.
Thus, we carry thee in our souls forever,
my seashell, my flower, my Beth.

CHAPTER 26

LETTERS

My wish came true.

I wished I hadn't a heart—and now it's gone. My heart was carved from my chest and it rests in Beth's casket underground. Now, I pray I hadn't the memory of a heart; the aching hollow is more painful than ever. Needles shred my insides at every moment of the day.

There are so many tears that my body cannot expel in time. They clog my throat and fill my lungs until I can't breathe. I'm left on Beth and Amy's bed, wailing and gasping for air and gripping the quilt in hopes that it could replace my heart. The vacancy is much too excruciating to bear and it steals most of my memory. I remember the pain sticking to my body, and Marmee trying to calm me down. Later, she tells me my face turned blue and my eyes unfocused. I apologize for bringing her more pain.

The sight of one's mother sobbing is unexplainable anguish. A woman so strong, capable, and known for keeping the house intact has lost a chunk of her heart. The house is nothing but a shadow. Happiness flees and sadness remains. Often, the only sounds are crying.

I can't bring myself to leave my bedroom. Most of my time is spent staring out of the window as I sit curled in a rocking chair. Hannah and Marmee make a routine of checking on me; mournful letters from the town gather in overwhelming piles that I end up tossing into the fire. These people mean well, but I cannot bear confronting the world—a world without Beth. I can't. It's too much.

On a gloomy, cold evening, Marmee knocks on the bedroom door. "Jo?"

"Yes?" I ask in a thin voice, for I'd just finished my third crying fit of the day.

"There's a letter for you."

"Is it from Amy?"

"No, dear."

"Meg?"

"No, dear."

"The Laurences?"

She sighs. "No."

"Then please toss it into the fire."

Marmee knows and understands my shutting out of the world until I'm ready. She doesn't push me. But I sense her lingering.

"It's... it's from Beth."

I jolt, turning in the chair to see Marmee's sorrowful gaze on me. She sets a small box and envelope on my bed, then shuts the door. A letter—from Beth? A fresh wave of grief curls around my gut as I remember the afternoon she requested time alone with John. She had him write letters.

I lower myself onto the bed and open the envelope with trembling hands. *Wait.* I should let more days pass. This is the last time Beth will speak to me. When I open this letter, nothing she ever said will be new to me again. Beth still lives in this envelope.

"No," I whisper, new tears falling. "Not yet."

I tuck the letter and box into my nightstand. Once I read it, she's gone forever. My brain does not dictate what comes next. My limbs move wildly, sliding on boots, a Sontag shawl, a cloak, a hat, and mittens. I fly out the door before Marmee or Father can question where I'm headed. I'm not sure. The library? The graveyard? I wander to Dovecote, the evening sun in the middle of its rapid descent. I knock on the door until John answers, his alarmed expression dimming into careful grief.

"Jo."

"Where's Meg?"

A figure appears behind him. I haven't seen her since the funeral and it isn't until I see her thin face shadowed with pain do I regret the decision. I abandoned her the way I abandoned Beth. Regret shudders through me as I fly to her; she welcomes my embrace.

"I'm sorry. I should—I'm sorry. I love you."

Meg hugs me tighter. Her whisper lands in my hair. "I love you. I love you." She pulls from the hug and holds my arms. "Did you read your letter?"

I shake my head. "I couldn't. Not yet."

The three of us sit around the fireplace as Daisy and Demi nap. For the first time since Beth, I welcome anyone into my soul. Beth wanted me to care for Mother and Father in the face of her demise, but slight resentment falls upon me; doesn't she know that my strength died with her?

I curl up beside Meg as if I'm a child, my head upon her bosom as she strokes my hair. I close my eyes and savor her heartbeat against my cheek—evidence of the life I take for granted.

"How do you do it?" I ask.

"Do what?"

"Keep going."

It takes her a moment to reply. Her chest rises and falls with steady breaths. "The twins. It helps—knowing I have children to live for."

John welcomes me to stay for dinner, and I oblige. It feels refreshing to move freely about a home without fear of bumping into constant reminders of Beth. I should never want those reminders to leave, but my soul must mend before I can bear more of it.

"Have you been writing to anyone?" Meg asks.

"I haven't been doing much of anything."

"What about your professor? Fritz? You talked of him an awful lot."

I shake my head as I set cutlery beside the plates. "I'm not thinking of such things these days."

She places a pot of soup in the center of the table, then places her hands on the back of a chair. I pause when she looks at me with such a vulnerable, worried expression. "Jo, I will say this and then nothing more so I won't be too motherly: Please, don't bury your heart. I know how you are with romance, but you don't have to be in love to be happy with someone. There can be life partners who make you feel fulfilled to the greatest extent. From what I've seen, your professor fills everything. He respects you. Listens to you. *Understands* you. If you stop having so many expectations you know you'll never meet, I think you'll be happier. Be vulnerable with him. See if he accepts it."

I feel a flutter, a memory of my heart, at the old spirit of my sister's motherly instructions. "I... don't know if I'm ready for that."

Meg offers a gentle smile. "That's okay, too."

I heed my sister's advice but remain adamant that such vulnerability is much too soon. Instead, it lifts my strength to start writing letters again.

February 10, 1870

Dearest Teddy,

I pray that your heart has healed and you are growing further into the man you are meant to be. I write this with the heaviest heart I've experienced. I wish I hadn't a heart at all, for Beth has died. I know that Hannah has already written to you, but I wish to include my own letter. This is an inconsolable pain, but I've got Mother, Father, Meg, the babies, and even John. You may believe it to go without saying, but I fear for Amy. She has a deeper heart than all of us, she merely doesn't like to show it. Please, Teddy. Console and comfort her. Hold and care for Amy, because this is a horrible time for her to be from family. Your heart may still be sore, but you are part of this family and it is a great comfort to know that you are there with her, even if the reason you sailed there is due to a fractured love. I will say this once and then pack it away for good. Writing me a letter to convince me to love you while my sister was on death's doorstep was selfish and insensitive. Let it be further proof that I don't make you into the most honorable of men.

My dear Teddy, I know you cared for Beth as a little sister. I am very sorry for your loss as well. I'm eager for the day you both return to us so we can be together and mourn as one. I miss you, my boy.

Ever Yours,
Jo March

The day I mail Teddy's letter, Hannah approaches me in my bedroom and says, "I know ye said to burn anything that wasn't from yer family or the Laurences, but I saved this one."

My stomach flutters at the sight of Fritz's name. I throw my arms around Hannah with a grateful silence.

JANUARY 18, 1870

Dear Miss Jo,

I've learned from Frau Kirke that your sister has passed. I want to tell you how sorry I am. I know that you care for her deeply. I wish I could have met her, but your descriptions of her and your family are strong—it is like I met her a thousand times. Please take care of yourself. I shall visit as soon as I am able—as long as you wish for me to. Write back when you are able, dear.

Sincerely,
Friedrich Bhaer

FEBRUARY 15, 1870

Dear Fritz,

Thank you for your letter. I didn't believe I had enough strength to write back; something possessed me to. It may very well be Beth's spirit wishing me to stop shutting out the world. This pain is worse than I could have thought possible. It's difficult to breathe, eat, and sleep knowing that Beth is not here. The world feels darker than it ever has before. I will tell you when it is right for you to visit. Tell Frau Kirke and the children I miss them dearly. And you, of course, I miss you every day.

Ever Yours,
Jo March

FEBRUARY 15, 1870

Dearest Amy,

I am sure that Laurie has told you. It hurts my soul that you aren't home with us, but perhaps it's for the better. It's ever so dreadful here, Amy. I cried for hours this morning when passing Beth's boots by the front door. There are constant reminders everywhere. I cannot escape them, and I am unsure whether it is bad to want to. Do tell me how you are. Is Laurie taking care of you? Tell me presently and I will wound him if he isn't. If you are able, I would like to describe an image for you to paint of Beth at the beach. I love and miss you so much, Amy.

Your Loving Sister,
Jo

MARCH 1, 1870

Sweet Jo,

Don't fret. Laurie is taking care of me. He is mending his reckless ways. Beth has humbled and sobered us both. I grieve terribly every day and wish to be home. It may be dreadful, with constant reminders, but Beth is a stranger to Europe. No one understands why I am so sad, why I'm crying at almost every moment of the day. At home, I could mourn with you all. There is only one person here who understands what I'm feeling. I fear life would be much darker if Laurie weren't here. Please, please do describe the image of Beth. I long to see her again and this is my closest way to do so. How are Mother and Father? Tell them I am safe and healthy. Their youngest daughter will be home soon and evermore protected in their arms. Kiss Meg and the babies for me. I love you all so much—more than a letter can ever capture.

Forever Yours,
Amy Curtis March

FEBRUARY 24, 1870

Dearest Jo,

Grief is a difficult battle. I pray that you feel better with each day. My heart aches as I imagine your suffering. I shall update you on Franz and Emil, considering you care for them deeply and are concerned for their paths in life. Ever since your departure, I dedicate every moment to them. Their health is good and their education improves. I have much confidence that they will succeed. They ask of you often and miss your comical methods of storytelling.

It pains me to think you are sad. Please remember our happy moments together to make you feel joy again, if but for a moment. While I treasure our adventurous evening at the tavern, I think often of the night we fled Miss Norton's party. It was a magnifi-

cent sight—you, sitting by the heating stove, in the most dashing sky-blue dress. Your unruly curls made me feel better about my constantly rumpled hair. We spoke of literature and poetry that night. Do tell, does this memory make you happy as it does me?

I keep your family's healing in my prayers.

Sincerely,
Friedrich Bhaer

"JO, HE LOVES YOU."

"Oh, don't say such a thing," I insist as I pace Dovecote's parlor. The words unsettle me greatly.

Meg gawks at me with Fritz's latest letter in hand. "*While I treasure our adventurous evening at the tavern, I think often of the night we fled Miss Norton's party,*" she recites. "*It was a magnificent sight—you, sitting by the heating stove, in the most dashing sky-blue dress.* And what happened at the tavern?" she asks with a suggestive smirk.

My cheeks redden. "Fun and dancing, that's all. But he thought the dress dashing—not me."

She rises. "Oh, please! He wouldn't give a second thought about the dress if not for you in it!"

Before I can respond, John appears in the doorway leading to the kitchen with both twins in his arms. "Darling, can you take Daisy? She's rather fussy."

"Yes, of course," says Meg as she moves to retrieve her daughter. When her husband disappears back into the kitchen, she notices my confused expression and lowers her voice. "We're dividing the housework now. I've been so busy making dresses for the theater, I found it unfair I had the entire load and I insisted we share."

I find a gentle smile sneaking up on me as I gather my niece in my arms. Upon working with Mrs. Kirke, I much preferred teaching boys, for many of the little girls cared for frilly deeds. I thought I would never want a daughter—until I watch Daisy bloom before my eyes. Her black hair has a soft curl to it and her dark eyes glisten with love.

Love dashes upon my being in a fickle manner. Grief joins me for breakfast, lunch, and dinner, and I soon feel incomplete without it. Moments of unfiltered joy settle upon me like an unfit puzzle piece. I still cannot bring myself to read Beth's letter, but I eventually realize that I cannot heal until I do. Beth is gone and she's not coming back. I have to start accepting that, no matter how painful.

Each day, my heart grows back bit by bit. My chest no longer sings with hollow agony; it is burdened with a prickle every time Demi or Daisy smile at me, every time Meg hugs me, and every time I receive a letter from Amy or Fritz. Teddy hasn't written to me and I fear that he detests me.

Marmee and I are at Dovecote one afternoon. I occupy the twins while my mother helps Meg complete dresses for an upcoming play.

"Have you thought of writing to Fritz yet?" Meg asks.

Marmee looks up. "I thought you just wrote to him?"

A smile sneaks up on my sister as she says, "No, she's debating whether to bare her heart to him."

"I need a heart first," I reply, twirling a strand of Daisy's hair around my finger. "And... I'm still unsure. I've been experimenting with all sorts of affections my entire life." I look at Meg. "I could never have what you and John have."

Her brows cinch with pity. "But—"

"I don't *want* what you two have," I explain, bouncing Daisy in my lap as my wishes pour out of me before I can tie myself together. "My entire life, I've tried to teach myself how to be romantic, but"—I exhale shakily—"I'm so tired of hating who I am because the world wants me to different. Romantic evenings in each other's arms. Loving him so much that he's the only person I live and breathe for—that's not me. It never has been and I don't want it to be. But... I-I should hate to be alone. I want—I want a companion. A partnership." I pull my niece closer and kiss her head. I cannot hold back the yearning tone of my voice. "And children. I want to be a mother. I will live and breathe for my children without hesitation."

Meg sits beside me and places a hand on my back. "All of that is possible."

Mother clears her throat and brushes a hand along the skirt of a dress. Her gaze lingers as if she's avoiding something.

"Marmee," I say, "what is it?"

"If I may be so frank—it is your choice, my dear, but I believe your sister's letter will help your decision."

CHAPTER 27

OLD, ANCIENT, DUSTY

My Sweet Jo,

How do I begin such a letter? I am dead, and you are not. It seems impossible to leave a parting message, even though we talk every day. My book is complete. My story is written, Jo. I am at rest, in my cottage, and you are still living. Your story is not over yet and you have many more chapters to write. Turn upon joyful memories in your sorrow. Prioritize our adventures; fight the pain until it falls. Although my life's run is short, it has been filled with a thousand lifetimes' worth of love, beauty, and wisdom. I'm no source of endless knowledge and wisdom, unlike Marmee, but my life and death leave me with these two pieces of advice I think my fiery Jo should follow.

1. Forgive. Forgive those who have wronged you or someone you love. Most importantly, forgive yourself. You are too tough on yourself, dear. You will be happier when you start being nicer to yourself.

2. Love. I know you have conflicted feelings about this topic. But I don't mean romance. I mean it in its simplest terms: love. It doesn't have to be sentimental, but let yourself love others. You have hardened your heart to many, and I think you will be happier if you love more.

I hope I don't sound judgmental. You have always remained my inspiration. You're so strong and passionate about what you adore. Your ambition is admirable. Writing is and has always been a vital piece of you. I beg that you do not give it up, for I know the happiness and pride it brings you. You believed your writing is the biggest contribution to the family, but you're the best contribution. You, and you alone. I guess I won't ramble anymore. I only want you to be happy—and dying will mean I can't help with that anymore. But I want you to know that I'm okay. You haven't failed; God does what He wants. Let the memories be written so they can last forever. I will carry our time at the beach in my immortal heart. I had Papa create the seashell you held to my eyes into a necklace to wear. You have been the best seashell a person can have. Now I will be yours. I love you, Jo.

Forever In Your Heart,
Beth

MARCH 20, 1870

Dear Fritz,

I write this with a trembling hand but a steady spirit. I am no swooning maiden nor a woman who has ever considered marriage nor a future as a housewife. It is relevant to admit that I have experimented my ways of romantic love with Laurie—only to discover that it is something I experience on a small scale, no matter the person. When we first met, I admired you greatly

212

because you're unlike anyone I've ever known. I'm learning my ways; I'm still growing. But there's one thing I understand to its full extent. My life is richer when you're in it. When I speak to you, I feel heard. When I confide in you, I feel understood. I believe we teach each other necessary lessons for a wholesome, fulfilled life. You know my passionate ways of life and, if you let me, I want to make you part of my passions. I want you to be my friend, my love, my teacher, my life partner—the one I'm tethered to for joy and sadness. Now, I may be honoring or humiliating myself. Your feelings shall determine the outcome.

Sincerely,
Jo March

"ANY MAIL?"

"No, dear," Hannah says with a sad expression.

Much time has passed since I sent Fritz such a vulnerable letter. Each day, I regret my decision and want to lash out at Meg for convincing me to do such a thing. But I control my temper and convince myself to let it go. I often pace in the garret, Beth's watchful seashell between my fingers. Her beloved spirit in the house pulses with life each day and grows stronger every time I remember the seashell around my neck. Nights fill with sorrow. Days fill with happy guises.

I spin my tales while in the depths of grief. No other emotional outlet proves to hold any kind of healing. My biggest drive is that Beth wants to hear about memories when I see her again. She craves my stories and successes and I won't let her down. Book ideas live in the very threads of life and I coax them out of hiding to gather in words.

I fall asleep one afternoon, exhausted from planning my

next book. My dreams dance little jigs in my head, giving me restful methods of travel. The voice lives in my dreams. It must be, for the voice is Teddy's—and he's in Europe.

"Jo!"

I flinch, the familiar sound throwing me into the conscious world. Indeed, my boy stands over me! "Teddy! You're back!" I leap off the chaise and launch into his arms. His laugh fills me with warmth and gratitude. Our friendship isn't ruined forever. He still cares for me—for us. I hug him extra tight.

"I'm back and I've got something to tell you."

"Wait." I pull from the hug, my hands on his shoulders. "First, I'm sorry."

I don't know why I say it. I hadn't planned to, but upon seeing him, it's the first word that pops into my mind. Guilt. Endless guilt and gratitude. Teddy's face pales, his brow furrowed. "Whatever for?"

"I feel I was harsh... when I turned you down. I could have been nicer. And my letter—"

Relief passes through his expression. He shakes his head. "Jo, please. You needn't apologize. I want to tell you *I'm* sorry."

My hands drop from his shoulders and I blink in response. "Really?"

"That, among some other things." He gestures to the couch and we sit. "I... you were right. We never made a good match—I see that now and I do thank you for being harsh. I needed it."

I clap my hand over his. "I'm so, so glad, my boy."

Teddy smiles. "You are my little writer. My best friend. The one I go to when I want to stir trouble and do something reckless."

"And the one you can count on to always tell you the truth," I add, poking his cheek.

"You make me into a better man as my friend, not my wife. I... I found someone else to do that."

I gasp and sit up straight. "You've gone and gotten married! To whom!"

He clears his throat. "That is—what I wanted to tell you."

His awkwardness gives me pause. "Teddy, why are you—"

"Amy," he blurts. "I married Amy."

My sister's name sends a jolt through me. Oh, how stupid I am! If Teddy's here, that means Amy is, too! I jump to my feet. "She's here? She's downstairs?"

"Yes, but, Jo—please don't be angry—"

"Angry?" I break in, halting my path at the top of the stairs. "Teddy, I care more about seeing my sister after two years. I don't care that you married her." Without waiting, I sprint down to the parlor. "*AMY!*"

There has never been such an abundance of love as the second I see Amy. We spot each other at the same moment and fly across the parlor. We greet each other as if soldiers returning from battle, latching onto each other in a dramatic embrace. Our crashing hug sends us toppling to the ground. The only sounds filtering about us are the squeaks of joy, grief, and gratitude.

"Jo," she cries.

"Amy," I sob.

The world blissfully slips away as my sister's love seeps into my body. It has been years since I saw my baby sister, and the warmth radiating through me and the tightness of my chest tells me that she held the missing pieces of my mourning heart. Beth left a permanent fracture in our family, but it takes only seconds of Amy's return to teach me how to stand again. I believed my tears to be gone forever, but my tears have never been as merry as they are now.

The news of Laurie marrying my sister surprises me —once the pleasant homecoming has worn off. It also doesn't take long to see the blissful match between them. They complement each other well and share a genuine love that cannot be denied.

After an hour of welcoming hugs and recantations of memories, a knock sounds upon the front door. I fly to it with a steady, full heart and yank open the door—there, in the threshold, stands Fritz. My smile wavers, replaced by a look of surprise.

"Fritz!"

He removes his hat and presses it to his heart. "Hi." After weeks of waiting for a response to my vulnerable letter, the last thing I imagined was his presence, *here*, unannounced.

A few silent beats pass. Someone's boisterous laugh echoes from inside, breaking our tension. His gaze extends past me, toward the parlor. "I see you haf a party."

His German accent sends a fluttering through my body. How I've missed the sound! "No, actually, we haven't." I throw a look behind me, my nerves dissipating. No matter the letter, my family has longed to meet him since I first mentioned him; if I act as though the letter doesn't exist... With a smile, I lurch forward and grab hold of his arm. "Only the family! Do come in, we're all very happy and would love for you to join."

"I don't wish to intrude."

"Please, you must join us." I take his hand and guide him into the parlor. "Father, Mother, this is my friend—Professor Friedrich Bhaer."

He appears hesitant at first, but the family welcomes him with kind greetings. Meg's wide eyes and Amy's confused brows turn my cheeks red. When Papa and Fritz begin chatting, slight humiliation crowds me. There is no inkling that Fritz received nor reacted to my letter. He can very well be playing along, only to plan on turning me down by the night's end.

Alas, no event hints at such a result. Fritz sits among the family as if he belongs, a sight that endears and frightens me terribly at once. It has been almost a year since seeing this esteemed professor I admire so much, and his sudden appearance tosses my wits to the wind.

Daisy and Demi take an immediate liking to him, climbing onto his lap and pulling his beard. I shoot Meg wide eyes and she flies over to pry off her children. Fritz and Papa fall into a discussion over religion, which dredges up an old memory I prefer to forget.

Meg's and Laurie's peeping faces in the kitchen intrigue me. I slip away to find them and Amy waiting for me.

"Josephine March," Amy scolds. "Who is this man and why is he in our house?"

I startle as Meg begins to undo my braid. "Well, it's Fritz. I've written to you about him before, haven't I?"

She plants her hands on her hips. "Yes, you have—but he's *here*? Why?"

Meg laughs as she runs her fingers through my curls, separating and fluffing. It's best to let her treat me like a doll. "He likes our Jo, Amy. Can't you tell?"

"Why, what makes you think such a thing?" Laurie asks in a protective manner.

"Well, neither of you read his letter telling Jo how he *swooned* over her when she—"

"Gigi!" I gasp.

"A love letter?" Amy wails. "Oh, Jo, why didn't you tell me?"

"I'm sorry, I-I just—" I whirl around to Meg, stopping her as she toys with my hair. My eyes grow wide with worry. I confess that, despite my longing for weeks for Fritz to be here, the easy adjustment of him with the family unsettles me greatly. A heavy stone weighs in my gut as, for some indecipherable reason, I want him to *go away*. "What's wrong with me?"

"What do you mean?" Meg asks as concern passes over her face.

Amy steps in front of me. "Nothing is wrong with you. Why—"

"No, no, no." I begin pacing and shake out my hands to rid the anxiety. "I've wanted to see him for months, but now that he's here, I want him gone."

"Why?" Amy asks. "He seems very agreeable."

"He is! There is nothing wrong with him. He's lovely and wonderful, but I'm used to his existence in my head and—and now he's *here* and it's real—"

"And you're scared," Meg finishes. She takes one of my shaking hands. "That man in there adores you. And that's *all* he is—just a man."

Laurie steps closer and regards me with a tender gaze, which sends relief and tranquility shuddering through me, for I no longer worry about the underlying intentions of such a look. "Now is usually when you get thorny and throw cold water," he explains. "Fight that urge." He shrugs. "Besides, I admit I rather like the old man, although I don't believe he's looked at me for longer than two seconds tonight."

My nerves begin to dissipate when he calls Fritz old. "Teddy! Don't call him old. He's only thirty-eight. He's not old."

My best friend's mischievous glint returns to his black eyes. "Old."

Meg steps behind me and begins twirling my hair into a quick, elegant bun at my nape and I plant a hand on my hip with a stern warning. "Teddy."

"Ancient."

"Now you're wishing for me to get cross."

"Dusty."

"Theodore!"

"*Elderly.*"

I lurch forward and fly a steady fist at his gut.

"Oh, goodness," Amy says as if watching two children bicker. She turns away with a comical shake of her head.

Laurie grabs his stomach and steadies himself. "I told you, you love him. I just helped you realize it."

My mouth falls. I fell right into his little trap without realizing it! I had believed him to be a grown man, but it is clear that the two of us will never be more than a couple of troublemaking children. I reach for Hannah's fresh basket of bread rolls and throw a piece at his head.

"You little devil!"

He fails to dodge it. "My dear! Your sister is abusing me!"

"You know better than to poke Jo," Amy states.

"Oi!" Hannah scolds from the dining room. "What are ye doing with my bread!"

I dart from the kitchen, through the dining room, and into the parlor to escape Teddy's revenge and Hannah's wrath. Meg's attempted bun unravels and my hair spills down my back. I spot Fritz standing by the fireplace and hide behind him.

"What is going on?" asks Marmee.

My fingers curl over Fritz's shoulder. "Teddy started it."

The professor half turns toward me with an amused smile. "If know anything about you, you had a hand in it."

"Are you on my side or not?" I ask with a hint of betrayal in my expression.

"Always, dear." He chuckles, but his humor soon falls away as his gaze rakes over my face in an earnest manner.

"What? Why are you looking at me like that?"

Fritz blinks, awakened from his reverie with a shy smile. "I... I haf not seen your hair long like this. That is all."

My face warms, for I sense that he likes the sight from his bashful and admirable expression. "Oh…"

"Jo, your skirt!" Meg wails.

I gasp as a flare of fire catches my eyes. Everyone leaps up in alarm and I stumble backward in the realization that the flames follow. My skirt burns with vigor and Fritz sheds his jacket and casts it upon the fabric. We smother the fire within seconds, but the humiliation burns still. It cannot get worse—until I lean down to situate my skirt while Fritz rises, causing our heads to knock together. We both flush and laugh, yet this is increasingly embarrassing by the moment. I can hear Amy and Laurie snorting with laughter, but Meg, ever my savior, swoops in and casts me away.

"Come, let us find you another skirt."

CHAPTER 28

LITTLE WRITER

Stories, without the death of the storyteller, never have an ending. Imagination leaps from reader to reader without relent. It is a pleasant reunion of sorts when my sisters and I gather at Dovecote. We sit with the overwhelming reminder of a beloved sister now gone, resulting in an hour of our silent tears. It is the first time we have mourned all together, as siblings, and it proves to be healing in more ways than one.

Amy tells us of the beautiful way in which Laurie loves her. It pleases me to see how she's humbled him greatly and how my sister finds a mutual, respectful life partner to guide and hold her. I knew that Teddy would discover a fine mistress for his house and indeed he has. They're a well-matched couple and I am eager to live alongside the rest of their story.

The process of bearing one's heart remains vulnerable throughout. Every night, I fear that my chapter with Fritz closes forever. Yet on the following day, he arrives to plant the seed of hope once more. He sits in our hospitality for a fortnight and mentions my letter not once. The question continues circling my sisters, Teddy, and me.

I distract my curious mind with my stories and thoughts of

Beth, but it proves difficult, for Fritz knocks on the front door and carries his usual air of compassion and desire. Mother and Father love having him around and they ask about him when he's not here.

The rain over the last week has been constant. While I cannot be happier that Amy is home and safe with the family, it's yet another adjustment; no one else is coming home. *Beth is not coming home.* The fulfillment that Amy's arrival gave me is the extent of this finalized family. We are unbalanced—and always will be.

I sit on the back porch with my legs tucked under me on a chilly, rainy afternoon. The bench swing sways me back and forth as I nurse a cup of tea and watch the storm create mud puddles in the garden. The grief is strong today. What if I forget what Beth's voice sounds like?

The back door creaks open. Fritz watches me with a somber expression, a folded quilt in hand. Droplets decorate his coat; he just arrived.

"Hi," he says.

"Hi," I croak, sniffling and wiping away lingering tears.

The floorboards groan as he walks closer and opens the blanket. He drapes it across my shoulders while lowering next to me, his left arm remaining around my shoulders.

"Is it Beth?"

"Yes." I fight the sob threatening to rise in my chest. "She loved to sit out here and watch the rain."

Tears spill over at my natural use of *love* in the past tense. I try to silence my crying, but Fritz tightens his hand on my arm and pulls me closer. I hear him mutter, *"It's okay,"* as I lean into him. While I often loathe grieving around anyone who isn't my family, the new comfort refreshes me. Fritz is the first person I feel safe with outside my family.

"It's peaceful," he eventually says, studying the rainfall. He points across the way. "Is that where Laurie lives?"

I lift my head. "Yes. The first time I met him, I was looking for Beth's cat, Whiskers. I was covered in mud, crawling around the garden—when Whiskers was at the Laurence house the whole time."

I can see the eight-year-old memory—Laurie standing at the fence he would later hop over hundreds of times to visit us, my crawling through the garden my sisters and I would tend to every year together. Perhaps Daisy can tend to Beth's usual plot. New traditions must be created.

"In this garden," I begin, "I searched for her cats and shoveled the walkways for her when it snowed. To Beth, there isn't an illness or sour mood that cats or a walk in the garden can't heal."

Fritz situates the quilt that falls from my shoulder. "Then maybe we get you a cat to soothe your pain."

I meet his solemn gaze. "A black one?"

His soft chuckle lifts my spirits. "Sure. A black one."

He gives no hint of whether he intends to speak of the letter. Right now, I'm content with that. My desire for him to stay in my life strengthens as I lean into his embrace and watch the storm. Romance is the one form of love that fades the quickest. I may not wish to celebrate anniversaries with Fritz or for him to sweep me off my feet and give me love letters tied to a rose, but what I feel is stronger, warmer, better. I feel peaceful longevity and enough drops of passion to sustain me many lifetimes.

But I need to know if he feels it, too. I can take it no longer.

On another rainy afternoon, after Fritz departs following an abundant lunch, I stomp into the foyer and slide on my rain boots.

"Where are you going?" Amy asks.

"To speak my truth," I reply, then add quietly, "even if my voice shakes."

There is no saying when Fritz will depart for good; I don't wish to find out by his sudden stop of visitation. I dash out into the rain and turn down the muddy road. His figure retreats farther from the house.

"Fritz!" I shout. The rain pelts against my face and sticks my clothes to my body. My skirt tangles in my legs as I run. It takes a couple of yelps for him to hear me. When he turns, he smiles. For a moment, confidence surges through me and I'm prepared to confront him. Until the muddy ground slips beneath my feet and leaves me splashing in a puddle in front of him. Before humiliation can settle, Fritz flinches and rushes closer to help, but loses his footing and falls before me in a heavy splash. The wind casts his umbrella away and we both burst into laughter. The tension in my gut eases as we sit in front of each other, drenched in mud.

"You never replied to my letter," I say. "Did you receive it?"

Fritz sobers, then wipes a hand on his coat before reaching inside. He shows me the letter for a moment before returning it to the protection of his pocket. "I read it many times."

"Why haven't you mentioned it?"

"I haf tried—every time I see you. But how does a man start a conversation when he can barely speak?"

As the rain spills around us, I feel myself sinking deeper into the mud. I shake my head. "I—I don't understand."

Fritz watches me with steady conviction, a hand to his heart and his eyes set on the little writer before him. "I am no writer like you, my dear. My words... you take them from me."

Still, he fails to explain whether this is good or bad. Still, I am unsure whether he wishes to be part of my passions. "I'm... I'm sorry."

"I'm not." He touches my cheek with his non-muddy hand and I try not to pull away—as such gestures make me uneasy.

> "But our love it was stronger by far than
> the love
> Of those who were older than we—
> Of many far wiser than we—
> And neither the angels in Heaven above
> Nor the demons down under the sea
> Can ever dissever my soul from the
> soul—"

I interject for us to finish the poem together: *"Of the beautiful Annabel Lee."*

"You read the rest of the poem," I state, my heart swelling.

His wet hair falls over his forehead. "You teach me as much as I teach you." His muddy fingers wrap around mine. "I want more adventures with you, Jo. All you say in your letter—I want that, too."

Blissfully, beautifully, covered in mud, Fritz kisses me with passionate tenderness that cannot accurately be set into words. Soft hearts must seek a home, and he is a sanctuary I heal and learn in. Our journey does not have an end.

And so, dear reader, while it remains a long time until I may visit my sweet Beth in her cottage, novels must have an end, even if temporarily. My family and I grow. Our mistakes are mendable. Our love is genuine. We dream in careless wonders that give us unique memories I treasure within a leather-bound book.

Years pass, people die, and babies are born. What is life if it is not cherished for greatness? I pray my readers harbor no hate for the liberties we brave March women possess, for we refuse to let borders conquer us.

"Dinner is almost ready," my husband informs me from the threshold of our bedroom. "Shall I tell the family you're writing? I'm sure they'd understand."

I turn to the window before me and spot the dozen little children romping through the yard. Not all have been nursed by my bosom, but they're all loved by my heart. To my left is the priceless painting of my Beth, standing on the beach with a gull perched on her hand, skirt and curly hair flying behind her. My heart twinges.

"No, my dear," I say, for no work can ever compare to the fulfillment of family. I slide off my pinafore and tuck my seashell necklace into my blouse to avoid little Ted's curious, tugging hands. "There will always be stories to write. I only have one family."

Before closing the book, I turn to the final page of my endless tale, *Little Writer,* and scribble two simple words.

THE END

Acknowledgments

None of this would have been possible if not for my mom and dad. I am truly the world's luckiest daughter to have such supportive, dedicated parents. I mean seriously—to have a mother and father who argue over who's prouder? I hit the jackpot. I love you both endlessly.

Gracie, you were the first person I told about this project and you were supportive since day one. You tolerated my spontaneous rants and sporadic messages about book covers. I'm so blessed to have a friend like you in my corner!

To my Llamasquad pals! I would be entirely lost in this industry without all of you. A special thank-you to Lenore Stutznegger and Catherine Bakewell!

A special-special thank-you to Nicole Aronis and Adriëlle Blaas. I don't even know how to begin thanking you two for being such amazing friends. Seriously. My gratitude for you two is bigger than words, which is ironic because we're all writers. I'm just very happy that you guys exist and I would travel across the world for you.

Kitty O'Rourke, thank you for enduring my panic emails and guiding me through the editing process! I'm so happy I found you and I'm forever grateful for the insight you've provided me.

Emily, thank you for always showing interest in my writing even if I'm not writing your favorite genre! I love you and thank you for being my sister.

Abigail, here's to many more writing retreats in the mountains!

Shannyn, thank you for existing and always being down to gossip about the period drama community. I'm so happy you're my friend.

Michaela, your excitement for this book has truly kept me going. Thank you!

My beta readers, thank you for your thoughts, reactions, and critiques!

Yenthe, thank you so much for bringing Jo to life with your stunning art! To have one of my artist icons draw my idea of Jo is a dream come true.

Lastly, thank you to Louisa May Alcott. This never would have happened if she didn't write *Little Women*. Louisa is one of the first classic authors I've read who wrote relentlessly and boldly. She didn't shy away from human flaws but instead embraced them. That's why everyone loves the March family—they're realistic. Louisa is also one of the few classic authors who was a proud abolitionist. I think she would enjoy my interpretation of her book.

About the Author

Marina Hill is a writer with a keen interest in all things undiscovered. She grew up in the New Jersey side of Philadelphia, watching Eagles games and roughhousing with her plethora of older brothers. She attended Baruch College in NYC and has over a dozen publications of her other works. If she isn't daydreaming about her next story, she's studying history or yearning to dash into the forest, build a farm, and never look back. Marina never lives in one spot for too long and loves to travel with her dog. *Little Writer* is her debut novel.

www.themarinahill.com

www.ingramcontent.com/pod-product-compliance
Lightning Source LLC
Chambersburg PA
CBHW010742310726
48971CB00010B/2918